By R. E. Toresen

Translated by Osa K. Bondhus

Dangerous Summer III

Part I:
A Question Of Alibi

Copyright: Text © 2007 by Eli B. Toresen
Published by PONY, Stabenfeldt Inc.
Cover photos: Fotograf Kallen
Cover layout: Stabenfeldt A/S
Translated by Osa K. Bondhus
Typeset by Roberta L. Melzl
Edited by Bobbie Chase
Printed in Germany 2007

ISBN 1-933343-50-8

Stabenfeldt, Inc.
457 North Main Street
Danbury, CT 06811
www.pony.us

Chapter 1

"Hey, Rachel, are you in there?"

Roger's voice made me jump. I had been in such a great mood, being in here with Núpur, my favorite horse at Sherwood Stable. School was finally out, and this was the first day of summer vacation. By some stroke of luck I had even been given permission to use Núpur for the entire afternoon. But now I could literally feel my good mood drain out of my body. Why did that creepy guy have to come in here and wreck my day? Wasn't it bad enough that I had to see him at home every day?

"I'm here," I answered reluctantly. "In Núpur's stall." I tried to look very busy, brushing away imaginary straws from the mane of this beautiful, Buckskin Icelandic horse whom I loved above everything in the world. I could only hope that Roger wouldn't stay very long. A couple of weeks ago he had come up with a crazy idea, to stay at the riding school for a whole day so that he and I could get to know each other better.

"You know, I really ought to learn more about my new stepdaughter's favorite hobby," he said with one of those slanted smiles of his. I detested that smile from the first time I met Roger Soto, and I certainly didn't have any desire to get to know him better. It was more than enough having to be around him at home every day. Needless to say, our day together at the stable hadn't exactly been the most productive, to put it mildly.

I heard him stop in the hallway right outside the stall, and quickly glanced up as I mumbled, "Hi."

"You've got to be President of the 'early risers junior society'," Roger said, laughing heartily. I didn't think it was particularly funny, but forced a little smile in an attempt to be polite.

"Lisa said hi, and she wanted me to ask you if you could get dinner started tonight," he said when he was finally done laughing. "We'll both be home around six. I'm going to a meeting, so it works out nicely for us to come home together."

"Sure, I'll fix dinner. No problem," I said, relieved that he would be leaving again right away. And I couldn't resist adding, "I don't mind making dinner for Mom. I've done that lots of times."

I was hoping he would take the hint, but he just smiled and said, "That's good. I'm sure you'll be a great housewife some day, sweetie-pie."

With that he turned and left, while I was fuming inside.

"Did you hear what that jerk said?" I asked Núpur, ruffling his mane. Núpur snorted happily as he tore off some straws of hay from the tray. "A great housewife! What a male chau... chauv... Dang it, I can't even remember the word!"

I heard the door open again, and the sound of somebody walking into the stable. I hoped it was my best friend, Bethany, because she and I had agreed to go for a ride together today. But it was two younger girls who were getting ready for their beginners' riding lesson. They chatted excitedly while struggling with saddles and bridles. I had to silence a chuckle, even though it wasn't that long ago since I was just as clumsy and inexperienced as they were.

Crash! One of the girls accidentally dropped the saddle with a bang. Goldie, the horse she was going to ride, didn't even move an ear. Goldie was an older, unruffled mare that was used to beginners, and took most things in stride. She just stood there patiently and quietly until the saddle and bridle were finally in place.

"Let me know if you need any help," I shouted over to the girls.

"Would you help me tighten the girth?" asked the smaller girl. "No matter how hard I pull, it's never tight enough. As soon as we get into the arena, Martin has to do it again."

"That's because the horse enlarges its belly with air," I explained as I tightened the girth another couple of notches. "They don't like to have anything tight around their bellies, see. There, I bet that'll do it," I said, giving the horse a pat on the neck.

After the two girls had left, each with a horse in tow through the stable door, I saddled up Núpur and got my helmet. People were coming and going the whole time I was getting ready, but still no sign of Bethany.

Finally I decided there was no point in waiting anymore. I led Núpur outside, checked his girth again, and swung myself into the saddle. Down at the arena the riding lesson had already started. Martin Olsen was standing in the middle, giving instructions to a group of more or less anxious riders. Martin was substituting for the stable owner, Jim Evans. Jim had received an offer to go to Alaska for a while, to work on a new oilrig that was being built. The salary they had offered him was apparently too good to refuse.

I rode over to the arena and called out to Martin, "If you see Bethany, would you please tell her that I'm going to the reservoir? I'll be riding toward the cove."

"Will do!" Martin called back. "Have a nice ride! And be careful crossing the road!"

"I will," I replied, slightly annoyed. Why did grown-ups always have to remind you about things you already knew? I was always careful crossing the road!

I directed Núpur down the hill toward the water. At the end of the hill was the main road, which frequently had quite a bit of traffic. To be on the safe side, I waited until there were no cars in sight before I let Núpur walk calmly across the asphalt. When we reached the grass on the other side, I made him go a little faster, at a light trot. I considered trying the tolt, but decided against it. The tolt, or running walk, is a four-beat gait that the Icelandic horse is known to be especially good at. Riders always talk about how great it feels, but I just can't seem to get it right. I must be doing something wrong; maybe my seat isn't good enough.

I took a deep breath, enjoying the wonderful sense of freedom I always have when I'm horseback riding. I bent forward and patted Núpur's strong, muscular neck.

"I wish you were mine!" I whispered with longing. "If you were, we'd go for a ride every single day, and you wouldn't need to deal with a bunch of lousy riders all the time, like those silly girls and boys who kick you in the sides and jerk your bit."

Deep down I knew I was being totally unfair. Most of the people who came to the riding school were considerate horse lovers who neither kicked the horses nor jerked their bits. To be truthful, the problem was more the fact that I disliked having to share Núpur with the others, regardless of how well they could ride.

Just imagine, if I could actually buy Núpur! That would be the ultimate thrill. But Núpur and I would probably be old retired citizens, at least, before I could scrape together enough money to afford him! At the moment I didn't have enough for even a fourth of the price of such a horse, and I wasn't in a position to save very much, either. When you're only thirteen, it's pretty much impossible to get a paid job after school. I had tried inquiring about a newspaper route, but they already had a long list of applicants waiting for an opening.

I sighed as I looked down at the reservoir with a blank stare. How different things had been only a few years ago. The time before Carl, my dad, lost control over his drinking, and Mom asked him to move out and filed for a divorce. My dad now lived in a studio apartment in a neighboring town.

"Hey, Rachel! Wait for me!"

Bethany's voice pulled me back to the present. I had been so absorbed by my own thoughts I hadn't even noticed that Núpur had switched from trotting to a very slow walk. He was strolling along at a snail's pace, grazing on the tufts of grass so temptingly close to the trail. I turned around and saw Bethany riding toward me. She was approaching at a gallop on Dreambell, another one of the riding school's horses. Dreambell was an Icelandic horse too, as were a lot of the horses at this particular stable.

"Did you fall asleep, or what?" asked Bethany with a laugh when she caught up with me. "I yelled a few times, but you just sat there like a dummy, so I thought maybe you'd dozed off. But of course, I can understand how dreadfully boring it must have been to go for a ride without me."

I had to laugh. "You're so modest!" I said, shaking my head. "Speaking of falling asleep, I don't think you're one to talk. Weren't we supposed to meet early today?"

"Sorry I'm so late," said Bethany. "I had to help my mom clean up after Steven. He went down to the kitchen before the rest of us got up this morning and decided to make pancakes by himself. He'd apparently seen some kids cooking on a TV show yesterday. Oh boy! You should have seen our kitchen! There was flour, sugar, and eggs everywhere, even in Dad's briefcase! Fortunately Steven hadn't gotten around to turning on the burner yet, because if he had, he probably would have set the house on fire! Anyway, I couldn't just leave my mom alone with such a big mess, so I helped her clean it up before I left. But I'll leave it to her to explain to that little monster what will happen to him if he tries something like that again!"

I laughed so hard I got tears in my eyes. Bethany's baby brother, Steven, is four years old, and let's just say he's a very creative and industrious child. He's always up and down, always into something, and ought to have a punch card for the emergency room, since he's constantly falling down from somewhere. Bethany once said that Dennis the Menace is an angel compared to Steven, and that she's going to start charging an extra high-risk fee for baby-sitting him.

But no matter how impossible Steven might be, I'm still envious of Bethany. It's not only because she has siblings, while I am an only child, but also because Bethany's parents are still together. Her dad, Richard Lawson, is the manager at the same Social Services office where my mom works. Her mom, Camille, is an elementary school teacher. I've known Bethany's parents since I was little, and they're very nice people.

But the main reason why I envy Bethany has four legs, is named Hawk, and will be arriving at the stable in a few days. It's Bethany's very own horse, which she received as a gift from her parents and her dad's sister. Bethany's aunt runs a stud farm back East, and she has this horse that she thought would be perfect for Bethany. Bethany went there to take a look at it, and she fell in love with the horse instantly. Over the last few weeks she's pretty much talked about nothing else. I think she's the luckiest girl in the world. Imagine getting a real horse as a gift! I let out a resigned sigh as I shook my head. Bethany looked searchingly at me and opened her mouth, probably to ask what was the matter. But before she had a chance to say anything, Dreambell suddenly let out a piercing neigh, jumped to the side and threw his head back. I could see the whites of his eyes. It looked like Dreambell had been scared out of his wits and was going to run off in a panic at any moment. Bethany had her hands full just trying to stay on his back. I pulled away with Núpur, not wanting him to get kicked or anything.

Bethany finally managed to get Dreambell under control. By then she and the horse were both sweaty, but just as suddenly as he had gone berserk, Dreambell was all calm again. He started nibbling grass as if nothing had happened.

Bethany patted him on the neck, asking confusedly, "Did you see what it was that scared him so much?"

I shook my head. "I didn't see anything. He just suddenly went crazy. Do you think he might have been stung by a wasp or something?"

"If so, it must have stung him on the muzzle," said Bethany. "I can't imagine a wasp being able to sting through the thick skin of a horse."

She slid out of the saddle and started examining Dreambell's muzzle closely, but didn't see anything unusual. To make quite sure, she checked his entire head, but found no sign of a sting anywhere.

Dreambell seemed happy with all the attention and started rubbing his head against Bethany's arm. She scratched him on the forehead before getting back in the saddle.

"Well, whatever it was that scared him, it's definitely gone now," she said. "Do you want to ride over to the cove? I'll race you!"

We let the horses wade around in the shallow waters of the cove for a while. Núpur was having a great time, while Dreambell seemed to be a little uneasy and unhappy. Bethany had to speak very firmly to him a couple of times in order to keep him in line.

"What's the matter with you? Are you getting temperamental in your old age?" she said with a light slap on his flank. "You can't behave like this in riding lessons, or nobody's going to want to ride you."

Dreambell merely snorted. He stomped his forelegs, making the water splatter around him. Dreambell had always been a little stubborn, but none of us had seen him behave like this before.

"I hope he's not getting sick," I said, looking worriedly at him. "It looks like something's bothering him."

"We'd better tell Martin when we get back," commented Bethany. "Just to be on the safe side."

Chapter 2

When we got back to the stable, however, we forgot all about Dreambell's strange behavior. Martin had very exciting news for Bethany.

"Your aunt called a little while ago," he told her. "She was wondering if we had a stall ready yet, and if it was okay for your horse to arrive the day after tomorrow."

"Woo hoo!" Bethany shouted for joy.

"But I told her no, of course," Martin continued, unruffled.

"Wh... what?" I saw the mischievous look in Martin's eyes, but apparently Bethany didn't. Her jaw practically dropped to the floor.

"No, we couldn't possibly take another horse around here for another month or so," continued Martin, putting on a grave face.

I had to turn away to stifle a chuckle. The expression on Bethany's face was almost worth paying for.

"But you can't... why can't I..." Words failed her.

By then Martin couldn't keep a straight face any longer. He burst out laughing, and I joined in.

Bethany just stood there staring at us, confused.

"I'm just kidding!" Martin managed to get out between gasps. "Of course I said your horse could come!"

"You... you...!" Bethany pretended to be furious, but she couldn't help laughing too.

"I assume you can manage to get the empty stall ready by tomorrow?" Martin asked with a smile.

"You bet!" said Bethany happily. "You'll help me, won't you Rachel?"

"Of course I will," I said, giving her my broadest smile, while I secretly tried to push that ugly green beast called Envy out of my stomach. It had curled up in there like a painful, hard lump.

Of course I was happy for Bethany, but that didn't stop me from wishing that I had my very own horse as well. Annoyed with myself, I shook off my impossible daydream and said to Bethany, "How about we clean out the stall first thing tomorrow morning, and then do the rest in the afternoon after taking a ride?" Then I turned toward Martin and asked, "Is it still okay to borrow Núpur and Dreambell tomorrow morning, like you said, Martin?"

Martin nodded. "As long as you only ride them lightly and come back by noon at the latest, it's fine. I need them for lessons in the afternoon."

Suddenly I came to think about Dreambell's nervous behavior earlier, and said, "Hey, Martin, there was something wrong with ..."

But before I could finish, a voice shouted, "Martin! Phone call! A man who says it's important – and urgent!"

Martin hurried off. "I'll see you later, girls. Would you put the horses in the stable, please? We're supposed to get some bad weather and a thunderstorm tonight," he shouted over his shoulder as he disappeared into his office.

As we put the horses back in their stalls, Bethany said, "I was hoping Martin would come back to the stable before we left. We didn't get to tell him about the way Dreambell was acting today."

"I'm sure it can wait," I reassured her. "Dreambell seems perfectly all right now, and whatever it was that bothered him may be gone by now. C'mon, let's go home. I'm starved, and besides, I promised to cook dinner tonight."

"All right," said Bethany. "See you tomorrow."

"Early!" I said admonishingly, "Don't forget!"

"I promise!" laughed Bethany, and she biked out of sight around the corner.

Chapter 3

I had just enough time to cook the pork chops and rice before Mom's car turned into the driveway. After we had eaten, Roger suggested that he and Mom go and see a movie that night.

"Could we go some other night, please?" asked Mom. "I'm so dead tired tonight, I really don't feel up to it."

But when it turned out that this was the last night the movie Roger wanted to see was scheduled to show, he started nagging her about going anyway. Mom finally suggested that he go and see it without her.

After much ado, Roger finally left. He looked kind of grumpy as he said goodbye, I thought, but when I mentioned it to Mom she just shrugged it off.

"Don't be so hard on Roger all the time," she said, "Sometimes I get the feeling that you're suspicious of everything he does."

"Well, I think it was kind of selfish of him to go alone," I said stubbornly.

"Wasn't it just as selfish of me to refuse to go?" said Mom calmly, but I could tell she was getting slightly annoyed.

"You're always defending that guy," I complained. "I wish you would wake up and see what he's really like!"

"I think I know more about what Roger is like than you do," she said, "And I know why you react so negatively toward him. You're afraid that if you allow yourself to like Roger, you'll be betraying your dad."

"That's the dumbest thing I ever heard!" I burst out angrily. "You are completely blinded by this guy! Some day he'll show his true colors, you just wait and see!"

With this melodramatic outburst, I ran up to my room and slammed the door. I sat down and waited, expecting my mom to come up and try to smooth things over, but she didn't.

After a while I felt pretty stupid sitting there, but there was no way I was going back down again. No matter what Mom said about Roger, I knew I was right about him.

After I had brushed my teeth and gone to bed, I thought about what my mom had said, about me feeling that I would betray Dad if I started liking Roger. How could she think that? I had no problem at all with my mom having a new husband! Not very much, anyway. But why did she have to fall for such an insufferable, obnoxious guy like Roger? Sure, I knew he acted friendly and charming when it suited him, but everything inside me told me that he was not to be trusted. How did we know what he was really doing on those business trips, for instance? Roger worked as a salesperson for some large medical firm, and would often be gone for more than a week at a time. Obviously, I thought it was wonderful to be rid of him. Whenever Roger was gone things went back to the way they used to be between Mom and me. And how could Mom be so sure that he didn't go straight to some other lady or something? He might even be married to someone else!

"C'mon, now you're being silly!" I said out loud, and jumped at the sound of my own voice. I was letting my imagination run wild, that's all. I'd rather think about something pleasant – Martin and the horses, for instance. Just imagine how different things would have been if Roger had been more like Martin: nice and easygoing, and really good with horses.

There I went again, getting irritated at Roger. As if that was going to do any good! I made an effort to focus on the horses.

This summer marked my fifth anniversary at Sherwood Stable. One of Bethany's cousins had been riding there at that time, and she was the one who'd convinced Bethany and me to go with her to the stable. It hadn't taken long before we were both 'bitten by the bug' and helplessly crazy about horses. Ever since then, Bethany had been fully determined to become a riding instructor or veterinarian when she grew up. As for me, I could see myself as a riding instructor, maybe, but never as a vet. Just the thought of blood and needles made me feel sick – and that wouldn't do at all for a veterinarian!

I felt totally nostalgic as I lay there thinking about my first feeble attempt at horseback riding, and I must have fallen asleep, because the next thing I heard was a loud rumble that made the window rattle. At first I didn't understand where the sound came from. I sat up in bed, confused. Was somebody shooting outside? But at the next rumble I realized that it was thunder, and a pretty bad thunderstorm at that. The horses! What would happen to them in this terrible weather? But then I remembered what Martin had said, that all the horses were to be taken inside because the weather forecast had warned of a bad thunderstorm. This reassured me enough to make me lie back down, but with the next powerful thunder, which was even worse than the first one, I shot right back up again. I jumped out of bed and scuffled toward the door to go and see if my mom was awake. A little comfort and reassurance would be kind of nice right now. I had always been afraid of thunder, even though I knew I was safe inside the house.

My hand was about to turn Mom's doorknob when I stopped short. What was I thinking? Roger was in there. Not on my life was I going to give him the pleasure of seeing me come running into their bedroom like a frightened little kid! So I snuck back into my own bed instead, pulling the covers up over my head. Every new roll of thunder made me cringe, but after a while the bangs got more and more distant, until finally the rain started pouring down. Soon it was over and all was quiet again outside. I congratulated myself for having held out through a severe thunderstorm all on my own for the very first time. I lay there looking out the window, dark clouds drifting by in the sky. The clouds gradually disappeared and I saw a beautiful, summery meadow. I was riding on Núpur, feeling happy that he was finally mine. Suddenly Bethany came riding toward me on a golden brown Icelandic horse.

"Aren't you going to congratulate me on my new horse?" I asked excitedly.

"That can't possibly be your horse," Bethany protested. "It's way too big for you!"

Surprised, I looked down and saw that I was sitting on an enormous, black, fullblood horse. It reared up and snorted so loudly that I could see the red parts of its nostrils. And suddenly I was frightened.

"What am I going to do, Bethany?" I yelled. But when I looked up, Bethany was gone. I was all alone, riding at a thundering gallop through a spooky, dark landscape full of cliffs. Then I glimpsed a figure in front of me. When it got closer, I saw it was Roger. He had an evil grin on his face, and I could see that he had long, sharp canine teeth, just like a vampire.

"I've got to get to know my stepdaughter properly," he hissed as he came steadily closer. I knew that if he reached me, it would be the end of me. As an unspeakable fear overcame me, I drove the horse to go faster. It pushed him backward, toward the edge of a cliff... further and further back. Then, with one last step, he toppled over the edge. I smiled triumphantly, but just as he fell, I saw that it wasn't Roger after all. It was my dad.

"Dad!" I screamed. "I didn't mean to do it!" But the only answer was an eerie and scary silence.

Chapter 4

I awoke with a start, adjusting to the daylight around me. As I sat up in bed, I felt dizzy and drowsy. What an awful nightmare! It made me shudder to think of the scary look on Roger's face when he came toward me in the dream. I hurried into the bathroom while the feeling of fear followed me like a shadow.

Not until I had showered and was blow-drying my hair did the dream let go of me, and I could finally laugh it off. It was just a stupid nightmare, nothing else, I told myself. And it was probably my punishment for having thought such mean things about Roger before I went to sleep. Maybe Mom was right – was I unconsciously trying to make him into a monster?

When I went downstairs, I ran into Mom. She gave me a warm smile and was evidently not mad at me anymore.

"Good morning, sweet-pea," she said. "I'm off to work now. We're expecting an extra money delivery this morning, and I don't know how early the car will be there."

"Extra money delivery?" I asked curiously. "Is something special going on?"

"No, we're just handing out some big state assistance payments tomorrow. We always have an extra money delivery the day before payments are issued. I'll see you tonight."

"Where's Roger?" I asked quickly.

"He has the day off, and he's still in bed."

Mom left, and I hurried into the kitchen. I was glad that Roger hadn't gotten up yet, because then maybe I could get out of the house before he showed up. Right now I couldn't bear the thought of having to talk to him.

I ate a quick breakfast and made myself a bag lunch, which I put in my mini-backpack. It was a small daypack decorated with horses, perfect for short outings. I'd received it as a reward from the PONY book club when I got another girl in my class to join the club.

There, now I just needed my watch. Where did I leave it again? Oh yes, I remembered. I left it on the bookshelf in the living room last night. I went into the living room and walked to the shelf, but there was no watch. That's funny...! Could Mom have moved it? If so, where would she have put it? I looked in all the places I could think of, both in the living room and in the kitchen, but my watch was nowhere to be found. Eventually I gave up. I would just have to continue looking for it when I got home later.

It was still quiet in the house when I left. I went into the garage, got my bike and punched in the code to close the garage door before taking off. It was all uphill from our house to the riding school, so it wasn't really a whole lot easier to bike than to walk, but the return trip was much faster and easier.

I parked my bike outside the stable and quickly went inside. Bethany was hard at work cleaning trash and debris out of the empty stall where Hawk was going to be staying.

"Hi!" she said cheerfully. "Is this what you call early?" I've been working for hours already!"

"Yeah, right! You can't fool me!" I said, smiling. "I saw your backside going up the hill just in front of me, so I doubt very much that you've been at it for more than two minutes!"

"All right, all right," laughed Bethany, "but at least I was first!"

"Congratulations," I said. "Maybe I should go and tell Martin to make a note of this sensation in the log book."

"Meanie!" snorted Bethany, making believe she was insulted and threatening me with the broom. I snatched the broom out of her hands and pretended to make a counter attack. Bethany took a step backward to get out of reach, but accidentally stumbled over her own feet and fell backward toward Dreambell's stall.

"I didn't know you were into ballet," I giggled. "Such elegant footwork would really look good on stage."

Bethany was trying to regain her balance, arms flailing. "I'm... Ouch!" she exclaimed, looking shocked as she retracted her arm. "Dreambell bit me!"

We stared accusingly at the perpetrator, who just stared unaffected back at us. Bethany rubbed her hand, but found that she had escaped with a only couple of bruises.

"It's not like Dreambell to bite," she said in a puzzled voice.

"Well, you might have scared him, the way you staggered toward him like a wounded penguin," I commented.

Bethany nodded, but I could tell that she wasn't totally convinced by this explanation.

As we stood there, Martin came in. Bethany told him right away that Dreambell had bitten her.

"And yesterday, during our ride, he suddenly threw a fit," I added.

When Martin had heard all the details, he got a serious look on his face.

"I think I'll call the vet and have him come and take a look at Dreambell," he said. "He has actually been a little touchy and irritable lately. I just haven't given it much thought before, with so many other things to worry about lately."

Bethany and I looked at each other.

"What do you mean?" Bethany asked.

"Oh, nothing in particular," said Martin elusively. "There's always something to worry about when you're running a riding school, but nothing you guys need to worry about. I'll go and call the vet right away."

"Well, there goes that ride," said Bethany after Martin had left.

"You can always run after Núpur and me," I teased, and when Bethany made a pouty face, I added, "I don't feel a bit sorry for you, just so you know. As of tomorrow you will have your very own horse and be able to ride all day if you want."

"You're right," said Bethany apologetically. "It won't hurt me to use my own two legs today, but you'll have to promise not to ride at a gallop. I can't run *that* fast!"

"Deal," I smiled, and for the umpteenth time I tried to ignore the sting of envy that shot through me every time the subject of Bethany's horse came up.

While Bethany and I cleaned out the last few things from Hawk's stall, I said, "Do you think the riding school has financial problems?" Bethany shrugged her shoulders.

"I have no idea. I know there were some rumors of that last year, but nothing happened, so I assumed it was just gossip."

"I really hope so," I said. "Just imagine, if the riding school had to shut down. That would be terrible!"

"No need to worry about that," said Martin's voice behind me. I jumped. He had returned from his office without us noticing.

"I'm sorry," I said, embarrassed. "We didn't mean to stick our noses into something that's none of our business."

"Oh, that's all right," said Martin. "I think it's natural that you're concerned about the future of the riding school. And it's true that we had some financial problems last year, but even though money is still somewhat tight, we're running with a profit right now, so there's no danger." Before Bethany and I could say anything, he continued, "I talked to the vet, but he doesn't have time to come until later tonight. I said it was okay. This isn't an emergency or anything. We're not even sure if there is anything wrong with Dreambell."

"Does that mean that I can ride him today after all?" asked Bethany excitedly.

"Well, I don't know..." Martin thought about it. "I'm not sure it's a good idea to ride him before the vet has checked him out. What if he throws a fit again while you're out there?"

"We won't ride very far," promised Bethany eagerly. "And if there is the tiniest indication that something's wrong, we'll come right back." Martin reluctantly agreed.

"But remember to be back before eleven thirty at the latest," he said. "I need Núpur for a couple of riding lessons, and Dreambell too, if he seems okay."

"I don't have a watch today," I said.

"No worries," said Bethany. "I do. With a new battery, even."

A little later we cheerfully took off on our ride. We didn't go to the reservoir this time, because Martin had asked us to stay away from traffic. Instead we rode up in the hills a short distance, to a nice, flat field where we often go galloping.

Dreambell didn't show any signs of acting up. Quite the opposite, he walked eagerly along the path. We gradually got more relaxed and allowed him to move into a fresh gallop. He took off like a storm, with Núpur right on his heels, and didn't seem to be bothered by anything at all.

Later we sat down and ate our sandwiches in the shade of a tree, while the horses grazed peacefully nearby. I fully enjoyed the freedom and the horses, and had no premonition about the drama that was about to unfold, only a few hours away.

Chapter 5

We handed off the horses a few minutes before eleven thirty.
Martin was relieved to hear that Dreambell had behaved like his
normal, old self again. Bethany and I left the horses with him
and then went into the stable to finish getting Hawk's stall all
nice and ready. When we were done, Bethany said she wanted
to go home for a while.

"I promised to look after Steven for a couple of hours, so
my mom can go shopping for some new clothes for herself. I
might as well get it over with, the sooner the better." I nodded
in agreement. Since I knew what Steven was like, I was not
a bit surprised that his mom would rather leave him at home
when she was going to try on clothes. The last time she took
him along on a shopping trip, he sneaked into a display window
and knocked over a mannequin, which in turn knocked down
almost the entire window display, creating a huge mess.

After Bethany was gone, I wondered if I should go home as
well. I didn't really want to. Most likely Roger was still there.
Instead I went down to the arena, where a lesson was going
on. Martin was just in the process of correcting a girl who was
riding Núpur. He seemed tense and stressed out, and I wondered
if he was still worried about Dreambell, even though the horse
looked just fine, walking along as obediently as a lamb.

I didn't recognize the girl riding Núpur as anyone I had
seen at the stable before. She looked kind of bad-tempered
and unhappy, I thought, and was evidently not paying much

attention to Martin's advice or instructions. After only a few minutes he had to correct her again.

"Morgan, don't jerk the reins, please!" he shouted. "It's very uncomfortable for the horse, and he doesn't understand your signals when you do that."

Morgan looked, if possible, even crankier than before, and I didn't expect to see much of her in the stable in the future. It didn't look like she had much interest in horses or riding at all. Most likely she had been talked into coming with a friend who was interested in horses.

I stood by the fence and watched the lesson until it was over. By then some riding students who were going to the next lesson had joined me. I waited to see if poor Núpur would be luckier with the next person riding him, and gave a sigh of relief when I saw Aaron, a boy in sixth grade, climb into the saddle. I knew that Aaron was very good with horses, so Núpur would be in good hands with him. But not in as good hands as mine, I thought to myself. Many of the riders were probably just as good at riding as I was, and of course, some of them were better, but I was sure nobody cared as much about Núpur as I did.

"If only I had the money, I would buy you in an instant," I whispered, suddenly lost in thought about how I would decorate Núpur's stall and paint a nice sign with his name on it, while everyone I knew would congratulate me on finally owning him. Unfortunately my dream was just about as likely to come true as me becoming an Olympic Show Jumping Champion. I could tell that I was putting myself into a bad mood by standing there wishing for the impossible, so I left the arena and walked back to the stable. After cleaning up Núpur's stall, I went on to sweeping the hallway. And when the riding lessons were all done, I helped sort the saddles and saddle pads, rinse the bits and lay everything out, ready to be cleaned. All of the horses except Rusty had gotten their halters on and had been taken out to the pasture. Rusty, on the other hand, stood tethered outside the stable, so I assumed someone was planning to ride him soon.

"Don't worry about it, I can do it tonight," Martin said when I asked if I should help him clean bits and bridles. "I have to be here waiting for the vet anyway. But if you would shovel the stalls down at the end for me, that would be great, because I didn't have time to do them all this morning."

"Sure," I said with a nod.

"Great!" said Martin. "Renee is in the office answering the phone today, so I'm going to take a ride on Rusty for a while. He hasn't had much exercise lately, so it might be good for both of us to get a little wind in our hair. This will be my last chance for a long time, because starting tomorrow we are completely booked with riding lessons every day."

With that Martin left, and I started shoveling the stalls. Afterwards I went up to the hayloft and did a little tidying up there as well. I felt really good about myself after I was all done, thinking Martin ought to let me use Núpur for at least two whole days after all this. But then I remembered him saying there would be riding lessons all day starting tomorrow, and my dream bubble burst instantly. Maybe I could ride him in the evening a little, instead? I decided to ask Martin about it when he came back.

My thoughts were interrupted by a voice, shouting, "Hello! Rachel, are you there?" I hurried down and was met by Renee. She's married to Jim and works at the office from twelve to four three days a week, answering phone calls, keeping the books, and that kind of stuff.

27

"I was supposed to tell you to go home right away," she said. "It was a man who called."

"That must have been Roger," I said. "Why do I have to get home? Did something happen?"

"He didn't say. All he said was to tell you to hurry home."

Chapter 6

By the time I got home and put my bike in the garage, I was worried sick. Nobody had ever called for me like that before, not even those times when I had gotten so wrapped up in my work at the stable that I forgot about dinner and time and everything.

I was out of breath when I flung the door open and rushed inside. Everything was quiet. I went into the living room. Roger was sitting in a chair, reading the newspaper.

"Hi," he said. "What's the big hurry? Is there a fire somewhere?"

"I came as fast as I could," I said. "What's happened?"

"Happened? What do you mean?" Roger looked at me quizzically.

"Why did you call and say I had to hurry home if nothing has happened?" I demanded.

"Me? Called? I don't know what you're talking about." Roger looked confused.

When I asked him about the message I'd gotten from Renee, Roger shook his head, saying, "I don't understand it. But I didn't call, that's for sure. There must have been a misunderstanding somehow. Are you sure the message was for you and not for one of the other girls in the stable?"

"Nobody else was there."

"Strange," said Roger.

I looked at him suspiciously. Was he telling the truth, or was he the one who had called? If he had, why would he have done it, just to deny it afterwards? That's too stupid. He was probably right; the whole thing must be a misunderstanding of some sort. I looked at my wrist, as I had done several times today. I wasn't used to not wearing my watch.

"What time is it?" I asked.

Roger looked at his watch. "Three forty-five. I'd better get some dinner started. Why don't you go and get changed, then I'll get you a glass of soda. You look like you could use a cold drink."

I took a quick shower and put on some jeans and a clean T-shirt. Then I went reluctantly back downstairs. I didn't really want to keep Roger company that much, but he was right about the cold drink, and a glass of soda sounded good.

I emptied the glass quickly. Then I tried to say in a casual tone to Roger, "If you don't mind, I think I'll go upstairs and relax in my room until Mom comes home." Roger nodded, but I thought he looked at me in a funny way as I got up and left the kitchen. Maybe he thought I was being rude for just leaving like that, and maybe he was right, but frankly, I didn't care. If he thought that I would like him just because he gave me a soda, he was sadly mistaken.

I must have fallen asleep almost instantly after I lay down on my bed, because the next thing I knew, somebody was shaking me awake, saying, "Rachel!" Wake up! Rachel, do you hear me?"

I sat up, groggy and confused. Then I came to with a start. Roger was standing in my room. What was he doing in here? And why did he look so perturbed? I was about to ask, but didn't get a chance to before he blurted it out.

"There's been an armed robbery at the Social Services office where Lisa works!"

I felt as if he had hit me in the stomach with a fist. Everything tensed up inside me and I gasped for air.

"Mom?" I managed to say. "Is she..."

"Lisa is all right," Roger said quickly. "I just talked to her. She called from the police station, because she wanted to let us know that she's okay, in case we heard about the robbery on the news."

Relief washed over me like a great wave. Mom was not hurt. But then I got all shaky again. Armed robbery, Roger had said. Did that mean that some lunatic had gone into the Social Services office and threatened my mom and the others with a sawed-off shotgun or something like that?

"What exactly did Mom say?" I demanded to know.

"Just that there were two robbers, and that it happened right before they were going to close for the day. I'm sure she'll tell us the rest when she gets home. She said she expected to be home in an hour or so."

I walked aimlessly around the house like a restless ghost, waiting for my mom to get home. I was constantly checking my watch, which I had now found again. It had been lying on the bookshelf, in plain sight. How I could have overlooked it this morning was a mystery to me. I must have been more tired than I thought.

Roger sat down with the newspaper again, as if nothing had happened. I couldn't understand how he could be so calm, and I told him so.

"I can assure you that I'm every bit as shocked and upset as you are," said Roger. "We're just dealing with it differently, that's all."

Finally we heard a car door being shut outside. I ran to the front door, just in time to see an unfamiliar gray car leave the driveway. Mom was walking toward me, and came inside. I threw my arms around her neck, totally numb with relief, because I hadn't really felt reassured that she was unharmed before I saw it with my own eyes.

Mom hugged me tight, and then carefully freed herself. "Ah, that was the second assault today," she said, smiling but looking a little pale. "I must say I much prefer this kind, though."

At this point Roger interrupted. "Rachel and I have been worried sick," he said, putting his arms around her while throwing a glance at me. I stared back at him with narrow eyes. Why couldn't Roger just for once keep a low profile? "Rachel and I have been worried sick!" As if! *I* had been worried sick, while *he* had been reading the paper! If only Mom knew how little he cared! I was fuming inside as we walked into the living room, but forgot all about my irritation when Mom started telling us what had happened a few hours earlier...

Chapter 7

"I'm sure glad this day is almost over," Richard said over his shoulder as he passed Lisa's station. Lisa nodded. It had been extraordinarily busy today, especially because it had been just the two of them.

"I'm sure glad we'll have more help tomorrow," Richard continued. "It'll be even busier with all the people coming in for their assistance payments." As he spoke, he went into the backroom.

Lisa had just finished helping an elderly lady, who was leaving. She glanced at her watch. Only seconds left until 4 pm. And no remaining visitors inside. Good, then she could go and lock the door. She walked around the counter, shutting the security trapdoor behind her. This was something she did automatically. But as she reached her hand out to put the key in the lock, two people suddenly rushed toward the door, pushing it open and forcing their way into the room. Lisa stared at the two figures in total shock. They were dressed alike, wearing thermal jackets and blue jeans. Their heads were covered by black ski masks, with holes for the eyes and mouth. But she couldn't see their eyes because they were wearing sunglasses as well. Both were carrying big sports bags. Actually they looked rather comical, except that Lisa felt no desire to laugh. She opened her mouth to scream, but no sound came out.

The tallest of the robbers said quickly, in broken English, "Don't make a sound, or I'll shoot." That's when Lisa noticed the gun he was holding in his right hand. He wielded the gun threateningly at her, and all she could think was, 'I'm going to faint.' But somehow she managed to stay on her feet. The other robber hadn't said a word. He grabbed her roughly by the arm. Just then, Richard came out from the backroom.

"Hey! What's going on here?" he said, shocked, as he started moving sideways toward his station.

"Touch that alarm, and you're dead!" hissed the robber who was holding the gun. Richard froze on the spot. In the meantime, the smaller of the two had wrestled the keys from Lisa and locked the door.

"Go into the backroom, both of you. Move it!" shouted the other one, wielding the gun back and forth between them.

Lisa and Richard were forced to open the vault and put the money into the bags the robbers had brought with them. Then they were pushed hard-handedly into the strong room. The robbers closed the door behind them. Just as the door slammed shut, the alarm sounded.

Chapter 8

"The robbers used my keys to unlock and escape through the backdoor, and by the time the police arrived, they were, of course, long gone."

Roger and I had listened quietly while Mom told us what happened, but now we practically bombarded her with questions. Finally Mom couldn't handle any more. She said she needed to go and lie down for a while. I offered to sit with her until she fell asleep, but Roger interrupted and said that *he* would do that. Mom didn't object, and they went upstairs. I stuck my tongue out at Roger's back as he disappeared through the door.

Mom got up again later in the evening, and we watched the news together. The robbery was headline news. We even got to see a video clip of the robbery. It was a recording from the security cameras mounted inside the Social Services office.

Suddenly I burst out spontaneously, "Look, Roger, they've got the exact same jacket as you have!" Roger shrugged his shoulders.

"So what? Half the city's walking around in those kinds of jackets this winter. That's probably why they chose them in the first place, so that nobody could recognize them by their clothes."

"Hush!" said Mom when they showed the video clip a second time. Roger and I fell silent. After the report was over and the news reporters had started talking about something else, Mom said thoughtfully, "Now that I've heard the robber's voice again, something occurs to me."

"What?" asked Roger quickly.

"I didn't really think he sounded like a true foreigner. It sounded more like he was faking the accent. Probably in order to make it harder to recognize him by his voice."

"You're probably right," said Roger. "The police aren't going to have an easy job solving this robbery, at least not if that video is all they have to go by. The robbers are so well masked they could be just about anybody!"

Mom and I agreed with him.

"I wonder if the robbers chose today by random, or if they somehow knew about the money delivery," pondered Mom.

"The police are probably working on the assumption that they knew about it," commented Roger. "I guess I should be glad I have an airtight alibi."

"What do you mean?" asked Mom, confused.

"Just what I'm saying," said Roger in a cheery voice. "Of course, I don't actually think anybody would seriously suspect me of robbery, but I am, after all, one of the few people who know that the Social Services office gets a money delivery the day before Assistance payments are issued. Which is why I'm glad Rachel can confirm that I was here when the robbery took place." Roger smiled at me.

I didn't return the smile, but I knew he was right. At four o'clock I was sitting in the kitchen drinking Coke while Roger was cooking dinner – no doubt about that.

It took me a long time to go to sleep that night, and when I finally did, I dreamed that everybody at the riding school was rummaging through my house, looking for my watch.

Somebody shut a closet door so hard that the whole house shook. I woke with a start. It wasn't a closet door I had heard, but the front door being shut. Then I heard footsteps. Somebody was coming up the stairs. I tensed up. What if it was a burglar? Or the robbers? What if they thought Mom would recognize them and tell the police?

I jumped out of bed, ran to the door, flung it open – and came face to face with Roger. I think we were both equally taken by surprise. I mumbled an apology about having thought it was a burglar, and then withdrew quickly back into my room. After that I lay in bed, pondering what Roger had been doing outside in the middle of the night.

Chapter 9

The next morning when I came down to the kitchen, I was surprised at first to see Mom there, but then I remembered that she wasn't going to work. The Social Services office had been temporarily closed after the robbery. Mom and Roger were sitting at the kitchen table drinking coffee and reading the paper.

"Hi," I said to my mom, paying no attention to Roger. "How's it going? Did you get some sleep?"

"Did I ever!" said Mom. "Roger talked me into taking a sleeping pill, and it did wonders. I slept like a rock!"

"You sure did," grinned Roger, glancing scornfully at me. "You didn't even hear the racket when Rachel attacked me last night."

"Attacked?" Mom looked questioningly at me, and I blushed. Why couldn't Roger keep his mouth shut? Wasn't it bad enough that I had made a fool of myself? Why did he have to go and rub it in?

"I woke up late at night and suddenly got this idea into my head that I hadn't locked my car," explained Roger. "When I came back after going out to check, Rachel came barging out of her room. Apparently she thought I was a burglar or something!" He gave a roar of laughter.

Mom must have seen that I didn't find it all that amusing, because she said quickly, "Roger will be taking me to the police station this morning. Richard and I have to go in for another round of questioning, in hopes that we might remember some more details about the robbers."

"Remember to mention that thing you said about the foreign accent sounding fake," I said.

"You bet," replied Mom. "It would be too bad if we led the police to focus their attention on somebody with a heavy foreign accent if the guy actually speaks fluent English." She hesitated, and then added, "The worst part is that I have a feeling there was something familiar about one of them. It was something about the guy who spoke with the accent."

"Probably just something you're imagining," said Roger. "More coffee, dear?"

When I biked up in front of the stable a little later, Bethany came running toward me.

"Isn't it terrible?" she said breathlessly. "How's your mom handling it? Dad was pretty shook up when he got home last night. He said it was completely unreal, even though it really happened."

"Mom was pretty out of it last night," I said. "But she's better today. You know that she and your dad will be talking to the police again today, right?"

Bethany nodded. "I heard that the robbers got away with over a hundred thousand dollars," she said. "I can't help but wonder if it was a coincidence that they struck on the day when there was all that money in the vault, or do you think they might have known?"

"I don't know – it's not exactly common knowledge," I said, just as Martin came out in the farmyard. I thought he looked kind of tired when he approached us and said hello. He had also heard the news about the robbery, and asked how my mom and Richard were doing. Martin knew Mom pretty well from the time when he and my Dad worked together at the bank. Evidently he and my dad were still keeping in touch with each other. Martin lost his job at the bank shortly after Dad did. Not because he had done anything wrong, but because the bank had laid off a whole bunch of people due to a so-called bank crisis. After that, Martin ended up taking all kinds of odd jobs here and there, so he was really happy when Jim Evans offered him the job as substitute manager of the riding school. Who knows? Maybe Martin will end up taking over the riding school altogether, if Jim keeps working on the oil platforms.

We talked about the robbery for a while, and then Martin said he had to get ready for lessons.

"Will Núpur be in lessons all day today?" I asked, hoping desperately that the answer would be no. But I was hoping in vain, although Martin promised I could borrow Núpur for a few hours the next day.

Just as Martin turned to go, Bethany asked, "Do you have any idea what time of day Hawk is arriving? I'm so excited, I can hardly wait!"

Martin smiled. "He's supposed to arrive sometime this morning," he said.

With everything that had happened the day before, I had totally forgotten all about Hawk coming that day. I felt almost ashamed about not remembering such an important event. Suddenly I remembered another thing I had almost forgotten all about. Martin was on his way into the stable when I called after him, "How did it go with Dreambell last night? Did the vet find anything wrong?"

"Not a thing. As far as he could tell, Dreambell is as healthy as a horse!" Martin answered humorously. I sighed with relief. That was at least one thing less to worry about.

Chapter 10

While we waited for the horse trailer to arrive with Hawk, Bethany and I helped Martin with a class of beginners. I led Núpur while a cute little girl, who was probably no more than seven years old, sat on his back, beaming with delight.

"Her parents want to buy her a small pony," Martin told me after class. "They just wanted to make sure she really liked riding first."

Some people sure are lucky, I thought to myself. Here is this tiny little thing, having everything handed to her – riding lessons, and her own pony. All she needs to do is think that it's fun.

"Life is so unfair," I mumbled.

"Did you say something?" asked Bethany.

I shook my head and forced the jealous thoughts out of my head. Truth be told, I had nothing to complain about. I had the opportunity to be around horses and to ride them almost every day. Even if it wasn't as often as I would have liked, it was still quite a bit. Not everybody was that lucky. My thoughts were interrupted by Bethany, who shouted, "Look! A truck is coming! Do you think it's Hawk?"

The truck came closer and, sure enough, it had a horse trailer behind it. Bethany gave a squeal of delight, scaring both Glonada, whom she was standing right next to, and the poor rider who clung to her back.

"Will you take it easy and not scare my students to death?" Martin asked sternly, but he couldn't help smiling. "Why don't you two go and greet the wonder?"

Bethany didn't need to be asked twice. She started sprinting toward the horse trailer with me at her heels. All my jealousy was gone. Right now I was only excited.

The driver was in the process of lowering the tailgate when we reached the truck. We could hear scraping and snorting noises from the inside the trailer.

"Can I go in and get him, please?" asked Bethany in suspense.

"Are you sure you know what to do?" asked the driver, and Bethany nodded eagerly.

She went into the trailer. I could hear her talking to the horse in there, and a minute later she appeared in the doorway with the horse on a lead rope. I stared at him. He was absolutely gorgeous, a dark bay horse with a full mane and tail.

Bethany smiled proudly as she started walking down the ramp with him. That's when it happened. Suddenly, Bethany's foot slipped on the ramp, and before she knew it, she was lying flat on her back in front of Hawk's legs. I almost didn't dare to look. What if he panicked and stepped on her? But Hawk didn't panic at all. He simply stopped and looked straight down at Bethany with his head tilted, as if he was wondering what kind of strange creature this was, who would go and lie down right in front of him.

I breathed a sigh of relief as Bethany got to her feet. She led Hawk carefully down onto the gravel and gave him a big hug. "Good horse!" she praised.

"Not so good girl," I said teasingly. "Couldn't you fall for him a little less literally?"

"Phew! I'd say you have more luck than sense," said the driver. He was more than a little shaken by Bethany's sudden fall. "It's a good thing your horse has such a calm temper," he added, while fastening the tailgate into driving position again. "If not, there's no telling how this might have ended."

When the truck driver had left, Bethany led Hawk into the stable so he could get familiar with the stall that would be his home from now on. He sniffed curiously at everything, checking out every nook and cranny, and seemed to settle in surprisingly fast. Bethany got out her grooming tools and started brushing him meticulously while I hung out by the door, watching her. Some of the other stable girls also stopped by to look at the new arrival, and two of them, Erin and Tanya, asked Bethany if she would like to join them on a ride in the afternoon.

Bethany glanced uncertainly at me, so I quickly said, "Of course you should go! I've got to go home soon anyway."

The last part wasn't really true, but I didn't want Bethany to feel that she had to skip the ride for my sake.

"Well, all right, then. I'd love to go," said Bethany. "I have to admit I'm dying to try Hawk on a real ride. And a little exercise will probably do him good after such a long trip, being all cooped up in a trailer."

Before she left with the others, Bethany and I agreed to meet at the stable again later in the afternoon. She was determined that I should try to ride Hawk, and of course I wanted to.

When I got home, I noticed that both cars were in the garage. That meant that Mom was back from the police station. I was eager to find out if she had any news about the case. I ran inside, happily unaware of the shock waiting for me there.

Mom was sitting in an armchair in the living room. Even though it was a warm day, she had a blanket wrapped around her. Her hands were shaking as she held tightly onto a steaming cup of tea. I could easily tell that she had been crying. Roger was standing by the window. He turned when I entered the room.

"Mom! What happened?" I asked anxiously.

"Don't bother your mom right now," said Roger gruffly. "She's had a shock and needs to be left alone."

I gave him a murderous look, and opened my mouth to give him an equally tart answer, but Mom spoke first.

"Roger, she has to find out sooner or later regardless," she said, and I heard a quiver in her voice.

"Find out what?" I asked, but at the same time something inside me wished she wouldn't tell me. It wasn't hard to tell that whatever she was about to say was going to be upsetting. "Does it have anything to do with the robbery?" I whispered. Mom nodded.

"The police found something in the backroom," she said quietly. "A silver necklace, which one of the robbers must have dropped."

"But how can a silver necklace be a clue?" I asked wonderingly. "Thousands of people walk around with silver jewelry."

"It wasn't just any necklace," said Mom despairingly. "I recognized it as soon as the police showed it to me." She swallowed heavily before she continued. "It was your dad's good luck charm!"

Chapter 11

At first I didn't think I would be going back to the stable that day, after the shock I had just received. But I needed to talk to someone. Mom had gone to bed with another sleeping pill and would most likely sleep until morning. Roger said she needed it, and for once I agreed with him.

Hawk was in his stall when I got to the stable, but Bethany wasn't around. She was probably at home having dinner. I walked out to the pastures and called Núpur. He trotted over to me and sniffed my hands excitedly.

"I'm sorry, baby, I don't have anything for you," I said, scratching him behind the ears. He sighed contentedly, but I realized that not even Núpur could cheer me up right now. After a while he got tired of being scratched, and returned to grazing with the other horses. I stood by the fence watching him for a while, and then went back to the stable. I didn't really want to talk to anyone but Bethany, so I decided to go upstairs to the hayloft to wait for her. It was warm, quiet, and peaceful up there. The voices from downstairs in the stable reached me as a steady hum, interrupted by laughter in between. I noticed that the winter blankets and covers, which I had stacked neatly in a pile last time I cleaned up here, were now scattered helter-skelter again. Just to have something to do, I started folding them up into an orderly stack while trying to not think about what had happened.

When I peeked down into the stable a little later, I saw to my relief that Bethany was there. I hurried downstairs to meet her.

Ten minutes later we were on our way to the reservoir. Bethany was riding Hawk, and I was walking. We didn't start talking until after we had crossed the highway and had gone into the fields. Then Bethany said resolutely, "Why don't I tether Hawk here, and then we can sit on the rock over there and talk. I can tell that something serious has happened."

"Didn't your dad tell you?" I asked in surprise.

Bethany shook her head. "The only thing Dad would say at the dinner table, was that the police had found an important clue in the case and that I had to talk to you if I wanted to know more."

We sat down, and then I told her what my mom had told me.

"...And of course my mom couldn't just keep quiet about the fact that she recognized the necklace. After all, she was the one who made it and gave it to Dad when they were engaged. My mom knew very well that Dad always wears his 'good luck charm,' as he likes to call it."

"But do you really think that your dad is a robber?" asked Bethany in disbelief.

"What else am I supposed to think?" I said desperately, "That necklace didn't walk into the backroom by itself. Mom said the police got a search warrant for Dad's apartment while she and Richard were waiting at the police station. She said the police were probably worried that she might warn Dad if they didn't act immediately."

"Do you think she would have?" Bethany looked inquisitively at me.

"Absolutely not!" I said indignantly. "Why would she help him if he did a despicable thing like that?

Suddenly I thought of what Roger had said: that not many people would know that the vault contained a particularly large amount of money that day. But Dad knew, of course, from before. Assistance payments were always issued on the same date every month, so he could easily have figured out that the day before would be a good day to rob the office.

"I wonder if the police found anything in his apartment," said Bethany with a pondering expression. We discussed the issue back and forth for a while, but it didn't help much with regard to my mood. Finally Hawk was tired of waiting and started neighing impatiently.

"You poor thing, did you think we forgot about you?" Bethany said lovingly as she walked over to him. He rubbed his muzzle against her arm while she scratched him on the forehead and behind the ears.

"Do you want to ride him now?" she asked, looking at me.

"Sure," I said, trying to look a little more enthusiastic than I felt.

We went down to the cove by the lake, and Bethany sat down on a rock to wait while I took Hawk for a short trail ride. If I hadn't been so preoccupied with sad thoughts, I would have thoroughly enjoyed it, because Hawk really was a wonderful riding horse. Spunky, but calm and sure-footed at the same time. "Almost as good as Núpur," I said quietly to myself.

When I got back to Bethany, I made sure to lavish Hawk with praise, and she beamed like the sun. We took turns riding him a few times, and then we headed back to the stable.

Chapter 12

On the evening news that night, we found out that a suspect in the robbery case had been taken into custody. In addition to the necklace that had been found at the scene of the crime, the police had confiscated a large amount of money at the suspect's home, they said.

Mom didn't actually sleep through until morning, as we were expecting. She came down to the living room right before the news started. After they were done talking about the robbery, she suddenly got up from the couch where she had sat down to watch the news. "I'm going to call the police," she said resolutely. "I want to know what Carl has told them."

It was a short phone call. "They wouldn't tell me anything," Mom said in frustration after she hung up. "The only thing they would confirm was that Carl had been arrested, and I already knew that much from the news."

"Well, what did you expect?" Roger said with a nonchalant shrug of the shoulders.

"A little more than what I got?" said Mom irritably. "But I'm not giving up yet. Tomorrow morning I'm going to the police station, and I'll demand to talk to Carl myself!"

The morning paper was full of news about the robbery. The confiscation of money at the suspect's home was front-page news, written in big, bold letters. Fortunately they didn't give any names, which I was very grateful for. The matter was bad enough without having everybody gawking and pointing at me, saying, "Do you see that girl? Her dad is the robber who was arrested!"

I shuddered at the very thought of it, and concentrated on the newspaper again. On page five there was a picture of the Chief of Police and an interview with him. That is, if you could call it an interview. He was asked about ten questions, and answered, "No comment," to eight of them. Mom and I almost butted heads in our effort to read it all, but we didn't really find out anything that we didn't already know. Roger was still in bed, and I didn't miss him.

After breakfast, which didn't take long since neither of us felt like eating much, Mom said, "I'm going to go to the police station now. And I'm not leaving there until I've found out what they know."

"You're going to leave before Roger gets up?" I asked, surprised.

Mom nodded. "He doesn't think I should talk to the police at all. He thinks it's better if we keep out of it as much as possible. Keep out of it? I was held at gunpoint, for heaven's sake! This case involves me, regardless of what Roger and the police say."

Mom was working herself up to the point of getting red in the face. I quickly told her that I thought she had every right to get involved.

"But Mom," I added, "There's something I don't understand. How could Dad, who has always been so kind and mild-mannered, even think of pointing a gun at you of all people? I know that all the evidence leads to him, but even so, I just can't believe it. Not about Dad!"

Mom looked distraught as she shook her head. By now she wasn't angry anymore, only tired and sad.

"I don't know what to tell you, sweetheart," she said,

"because I don't understand it any more than you do. The only explanation I can think of is that alcoholism and money troubles can drive people to do things they otherwise would never have dreamed of."

After Mom was gone, I thought about what she said, and decided she must be right. I sat around for quite a while, pondering. One moment I was willing to accept that my dad was guilty, and the next moment I was one hundred percent sure that he could never have done something like that. But if he wasn't the one, then who was? And if it was him, then who was his accomplice?

No, there was no use in speculating about it anymore. My head was already hurting from all the confusing thoughts, and the lack of sleep didn't make it any better.

I glanced at my watch. It was time for me to go to the stable. A vague memory of something was trying to surface from my subconscious, but it escaped again before I could figure out what it was. Oh well, if it was something important, I'd probably remember it sooner or later. Right now I was too tired to think.

Chapter 13

I met Martin at the door as I entered the stable. He was pale and didn't look very good.

"Hi," I said. "What did you do – party all night?"

He shook his head. "I think I'm coming down with something. Probably nothing serious, but I'm not feeling up to any lessons today, so I talked to Renee and asked her to cancel them all."

"I'm sorry," I said, a little more sympathetic. "Why don't you go home and go to bed? We'll take care of the horses."

"Thank you," said Martin gratefully. "That's so nice of you, and I think I'm going to accept. You can just leave the horses in the pasture today. But I'd appreciate it if you could check on their water supply. Oh, and Rachel, you can take Núpur for a ride, if you want."

"That's great!" I said. "Well, not that you're sick, of course. I meant it's great that I can have Núpur today."

"Then I'll leave everything to you and Bethany and the rest of the gang," said Martin, and with that he left.

"Oh, man – this is the good life, don't you think?" said Erin contentedly, throwing her arms out.

We were stopped in a meadow in the woods. Erin and Tanya had shown up just as Bethany and I were getting ready to go for a ride, and asked if they could come along. We said yes, of course. The only drawback was that Bethany and I couldn't talk privately as long as they were there. But it was actually nice to just talk about normal things for a change, and not about the robbery.

"How about a little race?" asked Bethany. "Across the meadow to the big boulder over there and back."

We all lined up, and Erin shouted, "Ready, set, GO!"

And off we went – that is, the three others took off, with Hawk in the lead. Núpur, however, didn't seem to understand what this was all about, because he just stood there as if nothing had happened. But when I urged him on, he finally got the point and took off after the others like an arrow. We caught up with Erin, who was riding Glonada, just as a plastic bag that had been lying on the ground got whirled up in the air by Hawk's hooves. Glonada spooked and stepped sideways. Fortunately, Erin managed to stay in the saddle, and Glonada stopped by a pile of broken and withering trees and branches.

The rest of us pulled up our horses and rode back to Erin, who was patting Glonada and speaking soothingly to her.

"Poor Glonada, did you get scared?" she said. "It's nothing dangerous, just a stupid old plast –"

Erin stopped suddenly, stretching her neck and peering at something inside the pile of branches.

"What is it? Do you see something?" asked Bethany, curious.

"There's something lying in there," said Erin. "It looks like a bundle of clothes."

"Maybe it's a body!" suggested Bethany, as always ready with a little sick humor.

"Don't be silly," laughed Erin. "Would you hold Glonada while I take a look, please?"

She crouched down and lifted up one of the branches. When she turned toward us again, she was completely serious. "There are two coats and some funny-looking stocking hats in there," she said. "You won't believe this, but I think we've just found the clothes that the robbers used! If so, I guess we'd better not touch them, in case there are fingerprints or something on them."

Bethany and I offered to stay behind and keep an eye on the spot while Erin and Tanya rode back to call the police. After they had gone, I asked Bethany to hold on to Núpur. Then I crouched down and lifted one of the branches to take a closer look at the clothes. Sure enough, there were two coats of the same kind that the robbers had used. And next to one of the coats was something that looked like it might be a ski mask. At least, it was not just an ordinary hat. But what was that, sticking out underneath one of the coats? Carefully, I reached out my hand and lifted the item slightly. It was a glove, and not just any kind of glove. I let go of the branch and got up.

"There are some gloves in there too," I said. "Riding gloves!"

"What about a gun?" asked Bethany excitedly.

I shook my head. "I didn't dare touch anything. But don't you think it's a little strange that my... that the robbers used riding gloves?"

I couldn't bring myself to say "dad." As long as I could say "the robbers," it felt less personal and threatening to me. I was still not able to grasp the idea that one of the thieves, who had used these clothes lying under the branches, might have been my own father.

Erin and Tanya soon returned with the police in tow. The police thanked us for our efforts and asked us to please ride away, because they were going to secure the area, take pictures, and I don't know what else. Reluctantly, and feeling somewhat put out, we rode over to the lake.

I told Erin and Tanya about the riding gloves I had discovered, and Erin said laughingly, "Robbery on horseback.

53

That would be something, huh? Just like in an old Western movie, where they leave their horses parked outside while they go inside and rob the bank."

"I think people would have noticed a couple of horses waiting outside the Social Services office," commented Tanya, totally serious.

"I'm just kidding, silly!" said Erin. "You don't need a horse to use riding gloves, of course."

"Yeah, who would the rider be?" laughed Bethany. "Martin, maybe?"

The others kept talking and joking, but I was no longer listening to them because something had just occurred to me. If Dad really was guilty in the robbery, then he must have had a friend along. And Martin had kept in touch with Dad, that much I knew. I also knew that Martin had been more or less unemployed for quite a while. What if he had accumulated a lot of debt, and was desperate for money? What if his little "coming down with something" was not a virus or sickness at all, but rather a guilty conscience because of what he had done?

I shook my head and laughed at myself. I was just letting my imagination run totally wild! Of course Martin wasn't a robber! The mere idea of it was completely ridiculous. Anybody could go and buy a pair of riding gloves. The robbers had used ski masks, too. That didn't mean they had to be skiers!

Chapter 14

Sleep didn't come easily that night. A thousand thoughts were swirling around in my head and I felt depressed and miserable. The whole time since I had returned from the stable earlier in the evening, I had nurtured a tiny, little hope that the case would be solved, and that Dad was innocent. One look at Mom was enough to crush that hope. She hadn't gotten to talk to Dad or the police. They had just referred her to Dad's court appointed defense attorney. He told her that Dad just kept insisting that he didn't remember anything at all from the day of the robbery. Dad either couldn't or wouldn't explain where the three thousand dollars the police found inside his closet had come from. The lawyer didn't hide the fact that things did not look good for Dad, and that it would be better for him to cooperate with the police and give them the name of his accomplice. But Dad had stubbornly held on to his claim that he didn't remember a thing, about neither a robbery nor any accomplice. I sighed and turned over in my bed. Who could Dad's accomplice be? What if it was someone I knew?

The scariest part was that the gun had not been found yet. It had not been among the clothes that Erin discovered in the woods. We learned that from the evening news. Nor had they found it at Dad's apartment. Mom thought that Dad or his accomplice had most likely thrown the gun into a lake or river or something, but I wasn't so sure about that.

The only good thing about the evening was that Mom and

Roger had a falling-out. I had no idea what they were arguing about, because I was in my room and only heard the boom of their angry voices. For a while I was tempted to sneak downstairs and listen in, but I couldn't bring myself to do it. The argument ended with Roger storming out of the house and driving away on screeching tires. By now it was almost twelve thirty, and he wasn't back yet. What if he didn't come back at all? But that was probably too much to hope for.

I startled when the phone suddenly rang inside Mom's bedroom. Who would be calling this late at night? The ringing stopped very quickly, which meant that Mom wasn't sleeping either. I listened tensely, and heard Mom shouting, "I couldn't care less!"

Then there was a bang, and I knew she had hung up on the caller by slamming the receiver down. Everything was quiet after that. I wondered if I should go in and ask if it was Roger who had called, but decided I'd better leave it alone.

After that I must have fallen asleep, because suddenly it was morning and my alarm clock was ringing by my ear.

I found a note in the kitchen:

Hi Rachel,
Hope you slept well. Went to work at 7. Dreading it, but I'll probably be all right. Coming home at normal time. Would you start some potatoes if you get home before me?
Love, Mom
P.S. Roger stayed over at a friend's in town. Don't know when he'll be home.

Well, he doesn't have to hurry for my sake, I thought as I sat down to have some breakfast. I wouldn't be sorry if I never saw him again in my life!

It was bustling with activity at the riding school when I got there. Martin was back again, a little pale still, but feeling much better, according to him. Núpur greeted me with happy neighing when I called him from the side of the pasture, and he eagerly chowed down the apple pieces I had brought for him.

"You're the best horse in the world," I told him affectionately, pulling his ears. "But today we won't be able to ride much, you and I. You poor thing will have to ride around the arena with a bunch of silly kids." I felt guilty as I looked around, but fortunately nobody had heard me. I'd better stop this stupid jealousy! Núpur was a school horse. Nothing could change that. I should be glad that I got to borrow him now and then.

While helping to get the horses ready for lessons, Bethany said fervently, "I have something very exciting to tell you, Rachel. It started when I forgot my riding helmet down in the pasture yesterday afternoon. I didn't remember I'd left it by the fence until late last night. And to top things off, I was stupid enough to tell my mom about it."

"What was so stupid about that?"

"Oh, you know, it got her all worked up, and she demanded that I bike to the stable and pick it up immediately," sighed Bethany. "I got a lecture about how I could be so irresponsible to leave an expensive riding helmet outside, and what if somebody were to steal it, and blah, blah, blah..."

"So, did you find the helmet?"

"Of course I did – it was right where I left it."

"And this was supposed to be really exciting?"

"No, silly! I haven't gotten to the exciting part yet. That was..." But she was interrupted by Martin who walked by and asked if we were going to get the last horses ready.

"Phew! Finally, there goes the last rider to the arena. Now we can talk again," Bethany said as she stroked a few hairs away from her forehead. "Let's go to the stable, then we can groom Hawk while we talk."

Hawk was the only horse that hadn't been outside in the night. Martin wanted him to get more familiar with his new stall first, before we took him through the next step, to be outside with a whole bunch of other horses that he didn't know yet.

We tethered Hawk outside the stable, grabbed a brush each, and started brushing him. Hawk looked like he was on cloud nine as he got massaged on two sides simultaneously.

"Now, where was I when we got interrupted?" asked Bethany.

"You were standing on the gravel over there," I said, pointing.

"Very funny!" Bethany stuck her tongue out at me. "I meant, of course, how far had I gotten in my dramatic story?"

"Not as far as an inch," I said cruelly. "The only thing you've told me is some long-winded story about your poor, lonesome riding helmet lying in the pasture. So, what was the exciting part?"

"Well, listen to this," continued Bethany. She lowered her voice to a dramatic whisper. "I had just picked up the helmet and was about to walk back to my bike, when suddenly a man came walking around the corner of the stable. He was wearing a cap and carrying a bag. He walked to the stable door, unlocked it, and went inside the stable."

"It was probably just Martin on his rounds, making sure everything was in order," I said impatiently.

"That's what I thought too at first, even though he disappeared too fast for me to see who it was. But I thought it very strange that he didn't turn on the light, because even though there was still some daylight left outside, it must have been pretty dark inside the stable."

"So what did you do?" I pressed.

"I walked over to the stable. I thought that since somebody was there, I might as well check on Hawk one last time and say goodnight to him. But do you know what?"

I shook my head.

"The door was locked – from the inside!"

I stared at her, befuddled. "How strange! Why would Martin lock himself inside the stable?"

"Don't ask me," said Bethany. "Anyway, I got really curious, so I hid behind the bushes closest to the stable, because I figured the guy would come out and go back the same way he came."

"So, did he?" By now I was engrossed in her story and totally forgot to brush Hawk. He snorted and tossed his head. Bethany scratched him distractedly on the forehead, as she shook her head.

"He was in there only a few minutes. When he came back out, he hurried down the road just a little ways, and then he turned into the woods over there."

She pointed. "So I only got a glimpse of his back. But I did notice one thing at least. When he came back out again and went down the road, it looked like the bag he was carrying was much lighter than when he went in!"

Chapter 15

"No, I give up. There is nothing here, other than the usual things!" I wiped the sweat off my forehead and looked around for Bethany. She was rummaging through the closet where we kept the saddle soap, leather oil, and various other things.

"We can't give up yet!" said Bethany stubbornly as she pulled her head out of the closet. She had dust in her hair and black stripes down her face.

"Good heavens, you should see yourself!" I laughed. "What are we going to say if someone comes in here and sees you like this?"

"Ha, if you think you look any better, you can think again," snorted Bethany. "You have sprigs of straw in your hair, and a big spider walking on your shoulder."

"Ugh!" I frantically brushed off both of my shoulders. "Is it gone?"

Bethany nodded. We had been searching the stable for about an hour, looking for whatever it was the mysterious intruder had left behind the night before. But the only thing we had found so far was a lot of dust, cobwebs, and Bethany's earmuffs, which she had lost sometime last winter. They were lying furthest back on a shelf with a bunch of tools, and didn't look very appealing anymore.

Before we started searching the stable, Bethany and I had let Hawk out in the pasture where he could run freely for a while, because the other horses were all being used in lessons or were gone on rides. Bethany glanced longingly at him more than once before we got back to the stable. She had initially planned to go with Erin and Tanya on a long ride today, but her curiosity was apparently stronger than the desire to ride, hence she had made up some story about having to go home and baby-sit her brother.

"Just think, you could have been on a wonderful ride right now instead of messing around in here," I said teasingly to Bethany.

"Don't remind me!" she sighed.

"Where do we look now?" I asked. "I think we've snooped through every nook and cranny in here."

"Well, there's still the hayloft. Come on!"

She climbed up the ladder, and I followed her reluctantly. I was tired of the whole game, and was convinced that there was nothing mysterious about the man Bethany had seen. It was probably just Martin who had left behind a tool or something. But when Bethany made up her mind about something, she was not to be budged.

"Honestly! Somebody has been here and messed up the stack of blankets and covers again!" I said, irritated, after I had gotten an overview of the loft. "This is the second time!" Bethany looked quizzically at me, and I told her how nicely I had cleaned up in here just the other day.

"But what was the point?" I grumbled. "They're all in a jumble again." Then suddenly a thought occurred to me.

"Do you think it could have been a blanket he had in the bag?" But Bethany wasn't listening anymore. She had started throwing aside all the blankets from the pile.

"Don't just stand there!" she said. "Come and help me, will you? I'll bet you ten bucks there's something hidden underneath here!"

I shook my head in resignation, but obediently began to help her. A moment later we had moved all the blankets out of the way and were staring at an old door, which apparently had been placed there instead of floorboards.

"Nothing there," I said, disappointed. "I'm tired of this now. We're just being silly!"

"Wait!" exclaimed Bethany with renewed eagerness. "Do you see these marks? It looks like this door has been lifted up fairly recently." She tried to lift it up with a rusty old screwdriver that she found under the blankets, but it just bent under the weight, so she had to give it up.

"You'll need something longer and heavier to lift the door with," I said. "Maybe a crowbar or something like that. I'll go downstairs and see what I can find on the tool shelf."

I jumped down the ladder and almost landed on Martin's head. He was so surprised, he roared in shock.

"Hey, what's the big hurry?" he said, looking questioningly at me. What's going on?"

I stiffened and didn't know what to say. It was too embarrassing to admit the truth – that we were searching the loft for something, but we didn't know what it was and it may not exist at all. Martin would just laugh at us and think we were being childish.

Then we heard Bethany's voice from the loft, "Rachel! You don't have to look anymore. My watch was up here, just like I thought."

"We... we... Bethany lost her watch," I stammered. "But I guess she found it."

"Well, that's good," said Martin. "I'd better hurry back to the arena; I was just coming in to get a lunging rope."

I was still standing in the same spot when he returned from the saddle room. He gave me another searching look, but didn't say anything. Then he left.

I breathed a deep sigh of relief. Then I hurried into the saddle room and grabbed the biggest and strongest screwdriver I could find.

Bethany was waiting impatiently for me to come back. "Is Martin gone?" she asked.

"Yeah, he went back to the arena," I said. "Thanks for getting me out of that! Man, I was totally paralyzed. I couldn't think of anything to say. I couldn't very well tell Martin that you were planning to break the floor up here! We don't even have the slightest bit of proof that anything is hidden here."

Bethany grabbed the screwdriver and stuck it in between the floorboards. Then she pushed, and the door made a creaking noise as it was raised. Dumbfounded, we looked into the hollow space between the door and the ceiling underneath. There was a red sports bag in there – chock full of paper money.

Chapter 16

"What are we going to do?" asked Bethany.

We stood in the pasture, pretending to be concentrating on Hawk. It had taken less than two minutes to put the floorboard back into place, pile the blankets and covers back over it in the same disorderly manner and replace the screwdriver on the tool shelf.

Then we had hurried out of the stable. Neither of us felt like being in there after what we had discovered. What started as an exciting game was no longer the slightest bit fun. Now it had turned scary instead.

"We have to tell the police," I said.

"But shouldn't we tell Martin first?"

"Are you crazy?" I burst out, alarmed. "If that's the money from the robbery, and it must be, then Martin has got to be the other robber, don't you realize that?"

Bethany stared at me as if I had suddenly grown two heads or something.

"Are you saying...?"

I nodded. "It actually makes sense," I said. "Martin has always kept in touch with... with my dad." I had to take a deep breath before I could continue. "They must have planned this together. I guess they must have been equally hard up for money."

"But Martin was here at the riding school that afternoon," objected Bethany.

I shook my head. "I remember seeing him riding out on Rusty that afternoon, and he wasn't back yet when I left."

Suddenly, something occurred to me. It was probably Martin who had called from a payphone or something to say that I had to hurry home. He probably didn't want anybody to be in the stable when he came back.

I told Bethany about this new idea, and she thought it sounded logical.

"That would explain why they used riding gloves too," she said enthusiastically. "Martin probably has several extra pairs of gloves lying around. And it would have been easy for him to ride out in the woods to hide the clothes they used. The only thing I don't understand is where he put Rusty during the robbery."

"Maybe he just tethered him to a tree," I suggested. "The Social Services office is actually not very far from the edge of the woods, so it probably wouldn't be too difficult."

"But if so, wouldn't the police have found the tracks from the horse?" objected Bethany. "After all, they did search the woods."

"Well, they may very well have seen horse tracks," I said. "But I bet it didn't occur to them that horse tracks would have anything to do with the robbery!"

No more than fifteen minutes after Bethany called, a gray car with policemen in plain clothes arrived. They first checked our story about the bag of money, and then they took Martin with them to the police station for questioning. They took pictures of the spot where the money was found, and then they took the money with them. We were told that there was about a hundred thousand dollars in the bag, which would be almost half of the loot from the robbery.

Everything took place in such a quiet and discreet manner that Bethany and I were about the only ones who knew what was happening.

The only ones who were asking questions were the riding students waiting for their instructor down at the arena. Bethany told them that Martin had suddenly taken ill again. We said the same thing to the other students who showed up later in the afternoon. We figured they would probably find out soon enough the truth about why Martin was gone.

Of course Jim and Renee had to be told about Martin. When we heard that it was impossible for Jim to come home any sooner than a week later, Bethany and I promised to take care of the horses in the meantime, feeding and exercising them. We knew we could count on Erin and Tanya to help us out when they found out what was going on.

When I got home there was another surprise waiting for me, but this one was a happy surprise.

"Roger has moved out!" said Mom.

"Has he really? Yippee!! " I shouted, forgetting all about the robbery. Then I stopped. "I'm sorry, I didn't mean..."

"Oh yes, you did," said Mom. "You've never liked Roger. I thought it would get better over time, but..."

"You're not saying it was my fault he moved out?" I said, shocked. "Oh, Mom, I didn't want that!"

Mom shook her head. "No, don't worry, it had nothing to do with you," she said, looking tired. "You didn't know, but over the last few weeks we have actually been arguing quite a bit. We're just way too different. It just wasn't working. Besides..."

She fell silent. I waited, but she didn't continue.

"Besides what?" I asked.

"Forget it, it was nothing," said Mom, getting up and tending to a pot on the stove.

While we ate, I told Mom about Martin and the robbery money. She was glad the case was being solved, but also very sad, because of Dad's involvement.

"I have to go back to the stable after dinner," I said. "Bethany and I have promised to take care of the horses until Jim comes home. But I want to watch the evening news first."

However, to our big surprise, the news didn't say a word about the money that had been found. All they said was that the police had some new leads in the case, and that a man was being held for questioning in connection with the new leads.

Bethany was just as surprised about this as I was, when I saw her at the stable again a little later.

"I was sure the money discovery would be headline news tonight, she said. "I don't understand why they want to keep that a secret, now that they have both of the robbers!"

"Maybe they want to keep it a secret until they find out where Martin has hidden the rest of the money," I suggested.

Erin and Tanya showed up while we were talking. They wondered if we had seen Martin, so we told them the whole story. They were both shocked, and as we had expected, they offered to help us with the horses until Jim came home.

After making sure all the horses were okay outside in the pasture, and everything was in order inside the stable, we decided to go for a ride. We saddled up Núpur, Hawk, Rusty and Dreambell. Then I locked the stable door and stuffed the key deep into my pocket.

"What time is it?" asked Erin.

"No idea," said Tanya. "I forgot my watch at home."

"It's five thirty," said Bethany.

Her voice interrupted a string of thought, of something nagging at the back of my memory, but now it slipped away from me again. It was something about a watch that was gone. Oh well, it probably wasn't very important.

We had a great ride. Núpur was spunky and in good form, and I thoroughly enjoyed sitting on his back, following his soft movements. After a while the others drove their horses into a tolt. I had tried to ride Núpur in tolt a few times, but I had never felt that he or I could do it properly. I decided to try again, and suddenly everything seemed to fall into place. I had a good seat, and Núpur moved rhythmically and nicely underneath me. It felt really great, and I didn't think about the robbery or the robbers for one second throughout the entire ride.

Dreambell, whom we had been so worried about earlier in the week, also seemed to be in good form, as happy and lively as a spring foal. There was no doubt that he was good again, that's for sure. It was almost eight o'clock when we got back to the stable. Everything was quiet and peaceful.

"I wonder if I should try to put Hawk into the pasture with the others tonight," said Bethany.

"It must be kind of boring for him to stand there all alone in the stable."

We kept a watchful eye on Hawk, who happily trotted into the pasture after Bethany had put a halter on him. I held my breath. Would the other horses accept him without a problem, or was there going to be a fight?

"Look!" said Bethany, grabbing my arm.

Glonada was trotting toward Hawk and stopped right in front of him. They stretched their muzzles forward, sniffing each other. Two minutes later they were grazing peacefully, side by side. None of the other horses paid any attention to Hawk at all.

"Nothing to worry about," I told Bethany. "He'll be just fine out here tonight."

We checked the water supply one more time, and walked along the fence to make sure everything was all right. To be on the safe side, we even counted the horses, not just once, but twice. Every one of them was there.

When we got into the stable, Erin and Tanya had started cleaning saddles and rinsing bits. As we all worked together, we discussed the robbery from every angle and perspective. Bethany was still the only one who knew that my own dad was one of the two people we were discussing, though I was pretty sure it was just a matter of time before this fact leaked out. Naturally, Erin and Tanya were mostly thinking about Martin, repeating over and over again how unbelievable it was that a man who was so gentle and good with horses could have done such an awful thing.

They asked how my mom was doing, and I was struck by horror when I suddenly realized that I had totally forgotten to ask her how her first day back at work since the robbery had been. I had been too preoccupied by my own rejoicing at the fact that Roger was out of the house. How could I have been so self-centered?

I promised myself to make it up to her when I got home.

After the saddles and bridles were all cleaned and ready, Erin and Tanya went home. Bethany and I made one last round to make sure everything in the stable was the way it should be. We were on our way out when Bethany suddenly remembered that a jacket she had used in the morning, was still lying up in the hayloft. I waited in the stable doorway while she ran upstairs to get it.

"Rachel! Come up here and see something!" she called from upstairs. "There's something funny here."

I climbed up the ladder. Bethany stood there with the jacket over her arm, pointing. "Look at that," she said.

At first I didn't understand what she meant, but then I saw it. The covers, which had been left in a disorderly pile by the ladder when the police drove away with Martin and the money, were now stacked neatly on top of the loose floor boards.

"Do you think Renee might have been up here and moved them?" I asked.

Bethany shook her head. "I kind of doubt it. There's something wrong here."

While Bethany ran back down to get the screwdriver, I started pushing the pile of covers out of the way. Soon Bethany had lifted the door up, and we both sat there motionless, staring.

"Am I seeing things?" whispered Bethany in disbelief.

She wasn't the only one having difficulty believing her own eyes. In the hollow space under the door, was a red bag, identical to the one we had found earlier in the day. Even the paper money was there!

Chapter 17

I was lying on my bed, fully dressed and staring at the ceiling. The shock and confusion was still overwhelming, it was like I could feel it all the way to the marrow. Mostly over the mysterious appearance of the money. Neither Bethany nor I could understand how it was possible, or what it meant. We finally decided there must have been a third accomplice in the picture. Somebody who had not been inside the Social Services office but had been helping out in the background, and who had evidently taken care of half of the loot. Because who else could have put the money there?

I had wondered why, if this was the case, the guy had not reacted to the fact that the rest of the money was missing. But Bethany speculated that maybe he would have just assumed that Martin hadn't had a chance to put the money there yet.

Bethany felt certain that he would come back to check on the hiding place, and was dead set on finding out who this mysterious third person was. Therefore she thought we should keep an eye on the stable and keep quiet about this new bag of money until we found out more.

"But we can't just keep watching the stable forever, can we?" I objected.

"He may not come back for several days. If he comes at all. I think we should tell the police."

"I'm willing to bet he's going to show up very soon," said Bethany. "Especially if he hears on the news that Martin has

71

been arrested and that the police have the rest of the money. Can't we at least keep watch in the stable tonight? If nothing happens, we can call the police tomorrow morning. Okay?"

Nobody was better at convincing people than Bethany when she put her mind to it, so I eventually gave in.

The second shock came when Mom turned on the TV to watch the 10 o'clock news before she went to bed. When the news reporters started talking about the robbery case, I thought first that I heard wrong.

"What did he say?" I gasped out loud.

Mom confirmed that nothing was wrong with my hearing, however. The man who had been brought in for questioning earlier in the day had been let go because there were no grounds for the police to keep him. I didn't understand how that was possible.

What if he was rude enough to come to the riding school tomorrow, as if nothing had happened? How was I going to stand meeting him, when I knew what he had done?

I wondered if Bethany had seen the news. Oh well, I'd soon find out when I met her at the stable at midnight. We both knew that our parents would never let us go out that late at night, so we had agreed to sneak out after our parents had gone to sleep. I yawned. Isn't it funny, that it is so hard to stay awake when you absolutely don't want to go to sleep? It wasn't even eleven o'clock yet. I couldn't risk sneaking out until at least eleven thirty, that much was definite.

But the time was passing extremely slowly... tick-tock, tick-tock... There was something I should try to remember, I felt, but what?

I was riding down the road at breakneck speed. There was something important I needed to reach. Oh yes, I had to hurry home. I had to be home before five to get Mom's sleeping pills, because otherwise she would find out that time was standing still. What time was it now? Oh, no! My watch was gone. Now I'd never get there in time. A big, dark shadow. A scary figure suddenly appeared right in front of my horse, making it rear up in fright.

"You're thirsty, right?" said a booming, frightening voice. "Drink now!"

"No!" I screamed in a panic. "I don't have time."

"You have all the time in the world," said the scary voice. "Don't you know that time stands still in dreamland? Don't you hear the clocks?"

The ringing of my alarm clock pulled me back to reality. In a daze, I fumbled for the stop button to turn it off. I peered at the digital numbers blinking toward me: 11:25.

Almost eleven thirty; time to go to the stable. I was sure glad I had been smart enough to set my alarm to be on the safe side. Otherwise I would probably have slept through the whole night.

I walked stealthily across the floor to the door and opened it a crack. Everything was quiet. As I reached the bottom of the stairs without having made a single creaking noise, I took a deep breath. The rest was a piece of cake.

Carefully, I got my bike out of the garage and rode away down the bike path. I wonder if Bethany will get there before me? I thought. She'd better not have fallen asleep or she'll miss the whole thing! But that wouldn't be like Bethany. What an awful nightmare I'd just had! It reminded me of something... but what was it? Then it finally occurred to me, and I almost rode my bike straight into the ditch with shock. It was like a lightbulb had come on inside my head. Suddenly I understood everything, even why there was money under the floorboards again.

I had been on the verge of the solution several times, without being able to see what was right in front of my nose. The thoughts were flying through my head at the speed of light. What about proof? Was it possible? Of course, it would be the simplest thing in the world!

I was so absorbed by my own thoughts that I almost ran right into Bethany, who came running toward me.

"Stop!" she whispered, agitated. "There's somebody behind the stable. Probably the villain. I heard the sound of breaking twigs a little while ago. Put your bike down, quick! We've got to hide!"

Before I had a chance to react, a big, dark figure appeared at the edge of the woods. It stopped for a moment and stood silently, on guard. Then it disappeared back into the woods.

"That's some villain, all right," I gasped, starting to giggle uncontrollably. "That was a deer!"

I hid my bike in the ditch. Then Bethany and I walked stealthily toward the stable, concealed by shrubs and trees. It was cloudy and pretty dark by now, but I had no problems making out the contours of the horses in the pasture. They were all standing around peacefully, their heads hanging, as they were probably sleeping.

I was itching to tell Bethany that I had finally figured out what was happening, but I didn't dare to talk too much, for fear that somebody was around and would hear us.

"Should we try to get into the stable?" Bethany breathed into my ear. "I have the keys in my pocket."

"Are you crazy? I whispered back with alarm. "What if somebody is in there already? I don't want to..."

I didn't get any further, because Bethany hissed, "Hush!" What was that?" She pulled me along, crouching down behind a bush.

There we sat, listening, but it must have been false alarm, because we didn't hear anything suspicious. After a while Bethany got up slowly, signaling for me to do the same. Then she started heading resolutely toward the stable.

"Stop!" I tried to whisper, because I'd much rather wait outside, between the bushes. It kind of felt a little safer. But Bethany was already way ahead of me and didn't hear what I said. Either that, or she didn't want to hear. There was nothing else for me to do than to follow her, stealthily.

When I got to the stable, Bethany stood by the door with a hand on the door handle. She turned to me. "That's funny," she whispered. "The door isn't locked."

I grabbed her by the arm to try and pull her back with me, but she pushed the door open and slipped inside. Hesitantly I followed her, closing the door quietly behind me.

Chapter 18

After we got inside the stable, we stood still for a moment in order to get our eyes accustomed to the dark. The stable was quiet and empty. The only thing we heard was the sound of our own breathing and heartbeats. At least I heard mine. My heart was pounding so hard I could feel it in my ears.

"Let's hide," whispered Bethany.

I agreed and pulled her with me toward the stall farthest back in the stable, which only contained a bunch of stacked hay bales.

"Don't be silly," snorted Bethany. "We won't see a thing in here. We should hide much nearer the ladder to the hayloft."

But we didn't get the chance. Suddenly we heard footsteps outside the stable. Whoever it was, was evidently taking for granted that the stable was empty and deserted, because they didn't make any effort to be quiet.

Bethany and I went into hiding in the stall we had been standing outside of. Neither of us dared even peek over the edge; we just crouched down, frightened, in the far corner of the stall. This was no longer exciting, it was creepy and scary and...

"I don't want to be here," whimpered Bethany.

"Hush!" I hissed. "What if he can hear us?"

The door made a slight creaking noise as it opened, then we heard it being shut again. The noise that followed was a faint, metallic kind of sound, which I couldn't put my finger on. For a moment it was completely quiet, and I barely dared to breathe.

At any moment I expected to hear footsteps coming toward the stall, and a voice saying, "Hey, what are you guys doing here?"

But when we finally heard the sound of footsteps again, they were not approaching us. They were going in the opposite direction, and we could hear creaking noises from the ladder up to the hayloft.

I made a jump as Bethany grabbed my arm. "I want to get out of here – before he comes back," she squeaked, and I could tell she was on the verge of tears from sheer fright.

I didn't feel a bit braver myself. It had all seemed so simple when we first planned to keep watch tonight, but now I would have given anything to be back in my warm, soft bed, safely away from whatever was happening here.

"What if he's got a gun with him?" whimpered Bethany quietly, and I felt my insides turn icy cold. The gun! I hadn't even thought about that once. I had just been so proud of myself for having figured out the answer to the mystery. Not for a moment had I thought that this might turn deadly. How stupid can you get?

I could feel the panic grow inside me. Quickly I grabbed hold of Bethany. "C'mon, let's get out of here," I whispered. If I had stopped to think it through, I would have realized that we were much safer where we were, but what little I had left of ability to think, was completely focused on one thing; getting out of there!

As quickly and quietly as we could, we sneaked toward the door. Just as I grabbed the door handle, we heard footsteps on the floor above us.

Run! was the signal my petrified brain gave, and I grabbed the door handle and pulled hard. The door didn't budge. It was locked! Bethany had realized the situation, and her hands were fumbling frantically to unlock the door. Of course it took twice as long that way.

"What the...!"

Heavy footsteps crossed the floor. There was a creak from the ladder.

"Help!" screamed Bethany. "Martin is coming!"

"It's not Martin," I said. "It's..."

"So! It's the two little Nancy Drews on the prowl, huh? Get away from the door!"

We obeyed, our legs trembling.

He just stood there, looking at us. It was too dark to see his eyes, but I could easily imagine the expression in them, and I was more afraid than I had ever been in my life.

"But... but..." said Bethany in disbelief. "It's..."

"Surprised, are you?" said Roger, laughing maliciously while he put down the bag he had been carrying.

"I'm not!" The words fell out of me before I knew I was going to say anything at all. I noticed that I was getting angry, and it was a better feeling than the panic I had just felt a moment ago. "I know you're the one who robbed the Social Services office – don't even try to deny it!"

"Don't be stupid!" said Roger. "You know perfectly well that I couldn't possibly have robbed any Social Services office. I was at home when it happened, remember?"

"How do you explain standing here with a bag full of money then?" I asked.

"I don't have to explain anything at all," said Roger. "This is just some money I won gambling, and I was planning to store it here so nobody would find out about it. As you may know, gambling isn't entirely legal in this state. But I guess I have to change my plans a little. I can't keep using the stable as a storage space. As soon as I disappear with this bag and another nice bit of money I've hidden in here, the police will only have the word of two hysterical, little girls that there has been any money here at all. And since one of the girls knows that I couldn't possibly have conducted any robbery – because I couldn't have been at the Social Services office and at home simultaneously, now, could I? – I don't have anything to fear. The police don't have anything on me at all."

Roger watched me spitefully. "You also know very well that your miserable father is the man who's guilty of the robbery," he snarled. "And so do the police. They have more than enough proof against him!"

"Proof that you planted, you mean!" I yelled. The thought of what he had done to my dad made me furious.

"What do you mean by that?" Roger's voice was dangerously mild.

"Oh, you think you're so clever, don't you?" I said. "But I know exactly how you did it – all of it."

"I don't believe you," said Roger scornfully, but I could tell he was starting to get uncomfortable.

"Everything was carefully planned. Even the part where you pretended to want to get to know me better and spent a whole day at the riding school. I guess that's when you made sure to get a print of the stable key, so that you could come here undisturbed and make a nice, safe little hiding place for the money, right?"

Roger didn't answer, and I continued, "That morning on the day of the robbery, I couldn't find my watch. Naturally, I thought I'd misplaced it somewhere, but that night it was back where I knew I had left it. I didn't think much of it at the time, but it's been nagging me at the back of my mind all along, until earlier tonight when I figured out how it all fit together."

Roger still didn't say a word, but he was clearly tensing up now.

"It was you who called and said that I had to hurry home.

And when I got home, you checked to make sure that I didn't have a clue what time it was. I don't know what you would have done if I had actually known. Postponed the robbery, maybe? Or taken the risk of not having an alibi?"

I didn't wait for any answer from Roger. I just continued in a furious tempo, "You said it was a quarter to four, but in reality it was a few minutes before three. Then you gave me a glass of Coke with some kind of quick acting sleeping pills or drug, and when I fell asleep, you went out and committed the robbery together with your friend, or whoever it was."

"Nobody you know," mumbled Roger. It was clear that he was shocked by my revelation.

"I don't care who it was. I'm sure the police can find out," I said. "What I don't understand is how you could do this to Mom!"

"I needed money!" Roger sounded completely desperate. "I've had some really bad luck with a few investments, and now I have a couple of hatchet men after me. They've given me a month to come up with the money. If not..."

"What's a hatchet man?" asked Bethany curiously.

I almost started. I had been so focused on Roger that I had forgotten she was there.

"Somebody who breaks your arms and legs, or worse, if you don't pay what you owe," said Roger bluntly.

"But why did you have to frame my dad for it?" I asked angrily.

"I couldn't afford to have the police keep investigating this forever. So I needed a scapegoat, and who better than some idiot who doesn't even know if it's day or night? It was the easiest thing in the world to get into his apartment and walk away with his supposed 'good luck charm'. Lisa mentioned once that she had handmade a necklace like that for him. So I knew it would be traced straight back to Carl. The only thing I wasn't sure of was if Lisa would tell them, or if she might decide to keep quiet about recognizing the necklace. But if she had, I could always have slipped an anonymous tip to the police."

"Lisa would never have kept quiet about something like that!" interrupted Bethany. "She's an honest soul, unlike certain others."

Roger ignored her. "It was just as easy to put money in his closet afterwards."

"But how could you know that Dad wouldn't have an alibi that day?" I asked, because that was something I had speculated about while I biked to the stable.

"As easy as pie," said Roger. "My friend sneaked into his apartment and mixed some sleeping medication into his morning orange juice. The dosage was big enough to guarantee that he would sleep all day."

Poor Dad! No wonder he didn't remember anything from the day of the robbery. "How could you be so calculating and totally heartless?" I asked Roger, but he just laughed.

"You could call it community service," he said. "A few years in prison might actually encourage your dad to start a new and better life."

Roger stopped for a moment, then he continued, "I was going to lock you up here in the stable until I got the money taken care of, but now that my alibi is ruined, I'm afraid that won't do anymore. I can't very well have you guys run off to the police and tattle."

"What... what are you going to do with us?" I asked in a whisper, regretting bitterly that I had been thoughtless enough to reveal what I knew.

"I don't know yet," Roger said. "I wasn't really prepared for this. I guess I'd better take you with me for the time being, until I can figure out what's the least risky way to get rid of you."

I felt like a bucket of cold water had been poured down my back. Get rid of us? What did he mean by that? Was he going to kill us? I suddenly felt sick and sweaty. Why didn't anybody come and interrupt this nightmare?

Frantically, I tried playing my last trump card. "It won't work – the police already know about you!"

I meant to say this in a strong, firm voice, but instead it came out as a pathetic squeak.

Roger laughed brutally. "Is that the best you can do?" he said sarcastically.

"But it's true!" said Bethany triumphantly. "The police were here yesterday and took both Martin and the money with them. But then they let him go, and suddenly there was a bunch of money under the floorboards again. Rachel and I thought there must be a third person involved, who had put the new money there, but now I realize it must have been the police. I bet they wanted to lure you into a trap!"

Roger started swearing heatedly. In a couple of long steps he was over by one of the stable windows, peering outside. Bethany and I took a few careful steps toward the door.

"Stay where you are!" commanded Roger and, terror-stricken, I saw something black and shimmering pointing at us from his right hand.

"The gun!" gasped Bethany.

"Exactly! So you two had better do as I say," hissed Roger.

He cast a quick glance out the window again, and was apparently reassured, because he came back and said, "There isn't anybody else around. If you have any more ridiculous fairy tales to tell, you'll have to wait until later. Right now we're going to get out of here."

He waved the gun menacingly. "Unlock the door!"

I tried my best, but my hand shook so violently that I couldn't do it. Bethany took over, and finally the door was opened. Roger signaled for us to go outside and followed close behind us, with the gun in one hand and the moneybag in the other.

The next moment we were blinded by a strong light, and a voice shouted, "Drop the gun and the bag, Soto, and put your hands above your head!"

Roger stood there like he was frozen to the spot. Then he roared, "Forget it!"

He grabbed me and held me in front of him as a shield, while he waved the gun and tried to hold on to the moneybag at the same time.

"Let the girl go and surrender, Soto! You don't have a chance," shouted the voice again.

"You keep your distance, or I'll shoot her!" screamed Roger menacingly. "You!" he said to Bethany, "you'll take the bag and come with us. Or else it'll be worse for your friend here!"

Bethany grabbed the bag without making a sound. But it was so heavy she dropped it right onto her shoes. "I can't carry it," she said.

"Then drag it along. Get moving!"

Roger made us walk toward the pasture. In a daze, I noticed that the horses had started stomping uneasily out there, reacting to this unusual commotion in the middle of the night.

"We're taking the shortcut across the field," he said. "My car is right over there." He gave me a push with the gun, and I felt sick with fear. I could barely move my legs, but he forced me to keep moving forward.

Suddenly Bethany called out, "Rachel, play Sleeping Lions!"

I knew what she meant. We had played that game with Steven and his friends many times. In this game most of the kids would lie down in sleeping positions, lying completely still, while one or two "hunters" would try to get them to move

83

by making them laugh. The hunters could not touch them in any way, only tell jokes or make funny noises. Her point was that I should throw myself down into a rolled-up sleeping position and become unmovable.

Roger's grip around me tensed, but before he could prevent it, I had made myself heavy as lead and dropped to the ground. Roger was so taken aback by this surprise move that he was unable to hold onto me. Then I saw a shimmering thing fly past me, and heard a shout from Bethany.

As I fell to the ground, I thought, he's going to shoot me. I curled up, closed my eyes, and waited for the bang, but it didn't come.

Instead I heard Bethany say triumphantly, "He dropped the gun, Rachel. I got it!"

I opened my eyes just in time to see Roger jump toward Bethany and reach for her arm. But Bethany was faster. She threw the gun as far as she could, and it flew through the air, landing behind a rock.

Roger cursed through gritted teeth, and stormed across the pasture. I don't know if he wanted to try and get the gun, or if he just wanted to get away. Either way, he didn't make it. Two policemen rushed out and wrestled him to the ground.

Bewildered, I tried to get up, but couldn't. Everything started spinning around me, and then the world went black. I heard a voice by my ear, saying something, but it didn't seem to have anything to do with me. The voice got gradually more distant, and then everything was quiet.

Chapter 19

"Hi, Rachel! How's it going?"

The unexpected voice made me turn with a start. I had been so deeply concentrated on brushing away mud spots from Núpur's back that I hadn't heard Martin coming.

"F-fine," I stammered, and felt my face turn red.

I had been dreading this meeting. After all, it was Bethany's and my fault that he had been arrested as a suspect in the robbery, and I didn't expect him to be happy about it.

It was Saturday; exactly 12 hours after a policeman picked me up from the ground where I had fainted as a result of all the strain. I had been pretty confused when I regained consciousness, and only had a vague memory of the police taking Roger to a waiting car and driving away with him.

All I was aware of was that Bethany and I sat in the backseat of another police car, holding onto each other. We both felt numb with relief and had a hard time believing that the nightmare was over. In the front seat was a policeman who asked us a lot of questions. We barely had the energy to answer them all, but managed at least to explain why we had been in the stable, and how I had discovered that Roger's alibi was a sham.

It caused quite a stir at home, because the policeman who drove us insisted on coming inside with me and waking up my mom. Naturally Mom was totally shocked to see me, because she thought I was safely asleep in my bed. But the police officer eventually managed to reassure her. As for me, I wasn't able to say anything at all. The officer, who wanted to inform her properly of what had happened, was made to wait in the living room while she helped me upstairs and put me to bed. I felt as if my arms and legs were filled with lead, and could barely move by myself. Mom said it was a reaction to the shock. She promised to come back and check on me as soon as she had talked to the policeman. And she probably did, but by then I was sound asleep and didn't notice a thing.

The next day I felt much better, except for feeling a little weak after the traumatic experience of the day before. Mom was considerably more depressed, which I guess was not so strange. After all, she had loved Roger, and then he went and betrayed her and lied to her in such an atrocious way.

I also found out the real reason why she had asked Roger to move out. Apparently, he had forged a power of attorney and used it to withdraw money from Mom's savings account. When Mom confronted him about it, he said he was sorry and that he would put back twice as much as the amount he had withdrawn. But Mom was not appeased by his words. She felt that she could not trust a man who went behind her back in this manner.

"I didn't have the heart to report to the police what he'd done," she said, "but now that I've found out what a miserable scoundrel there is hiding behind his charming facade, I've changed my mind. He's going to have to answer for the amount he stole from me too, in addition to the robbery and his attack on you. I will never forgive that beast for assaulting you," she added and gave me a big, teary-eyed hug. It felt so safe and good to have her arms around me.

The police had told Mom they'd arrested Roger's accomplice. Much to her astonishment, it turned out to be Roger's brother. He'd never even told her he had a brother!

According to the police Roger's gun had not actually been loaded when he grabbed Bethany and me.

"They don't think it was loaded during the robbery, either," she said, "which is a relief, even if I'll probably never be able to completely get over this ordeal. And it's going to take some time before I'll be able to trust a man again, that's for sure!" she added bitterly.

Everyone at the stable had heard what happened, and Bethany and I kept having to tell the story of that dramatic night over and over again. The only person we hadn't seen yet was Martin. But here he was, standing in front of me.

I scraped my foot on the floor in embarrassment while I mumbled, "Martin, I'm so sorry we made trouble for you. Are you very angry with us?" Martin laughed and ruffled my hair in a friendly gesture. "Not anymore," he said. "I was, to put it mildly, somewhat annoyed when the police came here and hauled me away because of some robbery I only knew through the media. You see, they didn't tell me about the money discovery at first, so I had absolutely no idea why they descended on me right out of the blue like that. But I eventually got to talk to an investigator who gave me the scoop on why I was a suspect, and then it wasn't so hard to understand anymore. Fortunately he was quickly convinced that I didn't know anything about the money, nor that I had been anywhere near the Social Services office at the time of the robbery."

"Are you saying he believed you just like that?" I asked as I scratched Núpur on the forehead. I had totally forgotten all about brushing him, and now he started getting impatient.

Martin laughed. "Not exactly. I was lucky enough to have an alibi – and in my case it was a true alibi! During the robbery I was actually riding with an old friend of mine – who even

87

happens to be a policeman. He has his own horse that he's boarding at my parent's place. We often go riding together, whenever we can fit it in to our busy schedules. I was sure lucky that he happened to come by that day, because otherwise things may have looked a lot worse."

I started brushing Núpur again. "But why did the police think of putting the money back again?" I asked curiously. "I didn't think to ask them about that yesterday."

"They were hoping that Carl's accomplice – because at that point they still believed that Carl was one of the robbers – would show up with the rest of the money."

Martin shook his head and patted Núpur, who totally reveled in all the attention. "Instead, you two crazies showed up," he said, with a mixture of resignation and admiration in his voice.

I nodded. Apparently it was a mystery to the police how we had managed to get into the stable without them seeing us. They had placed lookouts in the woods, in case the robber showed up to put the rest of the loot in the same hiding place, or to potentially pick up the money that had already been placed under the floorboards. And even so they didn't see us. They had both seen and heard Roger arrive at the stable, but had no idea that he was not alone in there, until they heard voices from inside. Their plan had been to storm the stable and grab him red-handed while he was placing the money with the rest of the loot. When they realized that he had taken two hostages, however, they had no choice but to wait until he showed up in the doorway with Bethany and me in tow.

"I'm sure glad it's over," I said as Bethany joined us.

"Have you thought about what you want to do with the reward?" asked Martin.

"Reward?" Bethany and I stared at him, without understanding.

"Have you two not heard that they offered several thousand dollars in reward to whoever gave information leading to the robbery case being solved?" asked Martin in disbelief.

We both shook our heads. This was news to us, so we had evidently missed that little detail. But if it was true, that might mean...

The grooming brush fell right out of my hand. It landed on my foot.

Bethany gave me a surprised look.

"Would you look after Núpur for a sec – I have to make a phone call," I said, sprinting into the office.

It rang and it rang. *Please be home, please-please-please*, I pleaded inside. Finally I heard the click, which meant that the receiver had been picked up.

"Mom, I've got to ask you something," I said even before she could say her name.

It turned into a pretty long conversation. When I came back out, Bethany was busy brushing Núpur's tail. Martin was not there anymore.

"Where's Martin?" I asked, breathless.

Bethany made an indication with her head.

"He went over to the pasture to get Rusty. Why?"

"He has to make a phone call for me."

Bethany looked like one big question mark when I, without any further explanation, sprinted toward the pasture, where Martin was walking toward me with Rusty on a lead rope.

"I talked to my mom," I told him breathlessly as soon as he was close enough, "and what you said about the reward is true. Mom had just been informed that the reward money will be paid to Bethany and me, fifty-fifty!"

"That's great – Congratulations!" said Martin warmly.

"You have definitely earned it, after what you two have been through."

I walked with him back toward the stable.

"Would you do me a favor, please?" I asked

"Well, I'll sure try, but I guess it depends on what it is," said Martin, looking questioningly at me.

"Will you call Jim and ask him if I can buy Núpur from him, please?"

"Jim is actually coming home for a little while next week. Could it wait until then?"

I shook my head so hard my hair was fluttering. "I can't stand to wait that long," I said. "Oh please, Martin!"

Martin agreed to try to get hold of Jim. "But remember," he said before he went inside to make the phone call, "I'm not at all sure if Jim will say yes, that he'll be willing to sell him. After all, Núpur is a young and good school horse."

I stayed behind with Rusty, whom I had been asked to groom while Martin went to make the phone call. Bethany eventually caught on to what was going on, and by now she was every bit as excited as I was.

While I brushed Rusty with long, slow strokes, I told Bethany about the other big news I had gotten while talking to my mom. Dad was released from jail, and had called her. He had finally admitted, both to himself and to a doctor who had talked to him while he was in jail, that he had a serious problem, and was finally planning to do something about it.

"I just hope he can do it," I told Bethany. "Mom has promised to support him as much as she can."

And who knows, I thought to myself. If things go well with Dad, maybe we could become a whole family again. It couldn't hurt to hope.

Martin was soon back again. He was walking slowly and looked so serious that my hope sank like lead in water. When he reached us, he put his hand on my arm and said, "I talked to Jim and I'm really sorry, but he said... YES!"

The last word came so unexpectedly that I jumped. Martin roared with laughter.

"You should have seen your face," he gasped. "It's the most tragic look I've seen in my whole life. I got you there, didn't I?"

"You mean... do you mean... he actually said yes?" I asked. I didn't know if I dared to believe it.

"Yep! Jim accepted the price you offered, too. Núpur is yours, as of today," said Martin with a big smile on his face. "And you can keep him in the stall where he currently lives."

"AWRIGHT!" I screamed, so loudly that poor Rusty reared up in surprise. I hurried to calm him down.

"We have to celebrate!" said Bethany, delighted.

"And how will you be celebrating?" asked Martin, as he finished grooming Rusty – something I had forgotten to do in all the commotion.

"With a ride, of course," said Bethany. "Is there a better way?"

"Definitely not," I said. "I'll be ready in a minute. I'm just going to get the saddle and get my horse ready. My horse! Do you hear that, Núpur? You are *my* horse now!"

A little later I was laughing out loud from sheer joy as Bethany and I rode our horses toward the lake. What an incredible day this had been! So much good news all at once! I almost wished I could put the moment into a frame, so I could keep it forever. But then I thought of all the exciting, wonderful days we had ahead of us, my horse and I. Today was only the beginning!

Part II:
A Question Of Revenge

Chapter 1

"C'mon, Núpur, we're in the lead!" I shouted, giving Núpur an encouraging pat on the neck.

"Only because you gave yourself a head start, you cheater!" said Bethany, who was following right at our heels as we rounded another tree.

"Did not!" I protested playfully. "You're just a slowpoke!"

It was Bethany who had suggested the race. "Let's see whose horse has the smoothest and fastest reaction," she said. "How about we ride zigzag between the trees, starting at the big rock over there and ending at the edge of the field? The last finisher treats me to an ice cream!"

"Well, then I hope you brought your wallet," I answered. "Ready, set, RIDE!"

The quick and unexpected start took Bethany by surprise. Núpur was twisting in and out of the trees so smoothly and lightly, it almost seemed like his hooves didn't touch the ground, and we had put several trees behind us before Bethany and Hawk had even started.

I had owned Núpur for a whole year now, but I still had to pinch myself sometimes to be sure that this beautiful, golden brown Icelandic horse really was mine. I had never, for a second, regretted buying him. Núpur was as gentle as a lamb, but could also be somewhat temperamental on occasion, so it was never boring to go for a ride with him.

"Falling asleep there, are you?"

I came to at the sound of Bethany's voice, and she wasn't behind me anymore. While I had gotten lost in thought, she had caught up alongside Núpur and me, and before I knew it, she and Hawk had slipped past us.

"I think I want orange-flavored ice cream dipped in chocolate!" she yelled over her shoulder as she and Hawk galloped toward the outskirts of the woods. She reined in Hawk as she turned and looked back at me, smiling. I smiled back at her, shaking my head in resignation. How could I have relinquished such a sure victory? But I didn't really care that much. Winning or losing wasn't what mattered to me. The important thing was that I was having a super-fun time with my very own horse and my best friend. And right now – remembering how difficult things had been last year – I felt like the luckiest girl in the world. It felt like I was on top of the world, and nothing could go wrong. Had I known then what the summer had in store for me, I may not have felt quite so high and mighty, but at that very moment, out there in the woods, life was simply wonderful.

It was on our way back that we got the first indication that something weird was going on. It started with a sound we heard, a steady hum, which was intermittently interrupted by a strange hiccup-resembling sound. Bethany pulled up on Hawk and said in a mystified voice, "What's that sound? Is it a sick tractor or something?"

The hum got louder. "I think it's an airplane," I said uncertainly. "A small propeller plane, by the sound of it."

"You're right! There it is!" shouted Bethany and pointed.

I looked up and spotted a tiny, little one-engine plane, which came flying toward us right above the treetops. The plane was heading straight for the field where we were standing.

The unfamiliar sound made Núpur uneasy, and he started stepping nervously about. I leaned forward and patted his neck comfortingly.

"Easy now, it's okay. Nothing to be afraid of." Núpur snorted quietly, as if he wasn't so sure about that.

Then, as the plane came right overhead, the pilot stepped on the gas and, at full throttle, it rose with a roar and another hiccup. Núpur got scared and reared up. The whole thing happened so fast that I slid right out of the saddle and landed on the ground behind him with a thump. Fortunately I wasn't hurt. Quickly I got to my feet, noticing to my relief that Núpur was not about to run away, which I had half expected him to do. He laid his ears back and stomped his feet uneasily, but remained where he was. I hurried over to him and grabbed hold of the reins.

"What an idiot!" burst Bethany out indignantly, pointing at the airplane, which disappeared in the distance. "Couldn't he have waited to rev the engine until he was a little further away? It almost looked like he tried to scare us on purpose."

I shook my head doubtfully.

"Why would he do that?" I objected, while I swung back into the saddle. "I think it's more likely... " Suddenly I stopped.

"Think what?" asked Bethany.

I didn't answer right away, because I had spotted something at the edge of the woods. "Don't turn around," I told Bethany in a low voice, "but I think somebody is watching us from the trees over there."

"Watching us? Are you kidding?" Bethany turned like a flash, just in time to catch a glimpse of the same thing I had spotted. Two men, dressed in something brown, possibly leather jackets, turned suddenly and sprinted into the woods. A moment later they were gone.

"How weird!" said Bethany. "Why would they run away like that? Do you think they're up to something?"

"I don't know what to think," I said, shrugging my shoulders. "When I first saw them, they were just standing there, staring at us."

"Good thing we're not going in that direction," said Bethany with a shudder.

"They were probably just some people going for a hike in the woods," I said. "And they probably stopped to look at the airplane, just as we did."

But if that's the case, I thought to myself, then why were they in such a hurry to get out of sight when they realized that we had seen them?

Chapter 2

"Are you coming straight to my place?" asked Bethany after we had taken care of the horses and were leaving the stable.

"No, I need to go by our house really quick to bring in the mail and see to a few other things first," I said. "Besides, I'd like to try to call the hotel where Mom and Dad are going to stay, just to see if they got there all right."

"It's kind of strange, isn't it?" said Bethany. "Last night they were here, and now they're in Canada."

I nodded. It was really strange to think that my parents were in a whole different country. And even more strange because I had never really thought that they would get back together again. As soon as Dad was released from jail he started attending local AA (Alcoholics Anonymous) meetings, and when Mom realized that he was serious about changing, she eventually asked him to move back home. Right now Mom and Dad were on a 2-week AA seminar in Canada. I was staying with Bethany while they were gone, because Mom didn't like the thought of me staying all alone in the house at night.

"Honestly, Mom, I'm not a little kid anymore," I protested, but Mom didn't budge, and to be honest, I was happy about that. I'm actually a little afraid of the dark.

Walking into my empty house, I was grateful that I didn't have to stay there all alone for two weeks. The silence seemed oppressive and totally different than usual. I'm often home alone after school, but that's different, because then I know somebody will be coming home in a couple of hours. In that case it's really nice to have the house to myself for a little while. But now, when I knew that nobody else would be around for two whole weeks, the silence got on my nerves. I suddenly wished I had asked Bethany to come with me.

"Oh, stop being such a baby!" I said to myself. Then I decided to turn on the CD player to get a little life into the house while I was looking for the toiletries I had forgotten to bring the day before. I turned on the stereo. It was set on radio, so it started in the middle of the news. The reporter was talking about some foreign politician who had been exposed for corruption. I reached my hand out to switch the system to CD, but the next news report made me stop in mid-motion.

"We've just received a message that the two prisoners who escaped from the State Prison last night are still on the loose," said the reporter in a dry, unaffected voice. "The fugitives are 30 year old Roger Soto and his 25 year old brother, Will Soto.

I dropped right down on a chair as I tried to take in what I had just heard. In the background the news reporter continued talking. He was describing Roger's and Will's appearances in detail, but I was unable to pay attention. Besides, I knew perfectly well what Roger looked like. And I would never forget the hateful, dark look in his eyes when he realized that I knew what he had done. It felt like icy cold fingers crawling up my spine, at the same time as I got flushed and hot in the face. The only thought I could focus on was, what if Roger came here to get revenge on me for having exposed him? What if he was already sneaking around the house this instant?

The thought made me get a move on. I ran to the bathroom as fast as I could, grabbed the things I needed and sprinted back downstairs. Two minutes later I biked at top speed over to Bethany's house. The whole time I couldn't help looking anxiously around, as if I expected Roger to suddenly jump out of the ground and attack me.

When I turned into the driveway outside Bethany's house, I left my bike lying on the ground and ran inside, slamming the front door so hard it made the house shake. Bethany's mom heard the commotion and came out from the living room, holding a book she was reading in one hand.

"Phew! I'm glad to see it's you!" she said with a smile, waving the book. "I almost thought that this scary story I'm reading had become reality!"

Then she looked searchingly at me, and became serious. "What's the matter?" she asked. "You look like you've been scared to death."

"The news..." I stammered. "They said... they said..."

Bethany's mom grabbed hold of my arm. "Has something happened to your parents?" she asked with a worried expression. "An airplane accident? An attack? I haven't listened to the news today."

I shook my head and quickly told her what had happened.

"I'm calling the police right away," said Bethany's mom firmly. "If there's any chance that Roger might come here, they're just going to have to keep an eye on you."

After a lot of back and forth, she was finally transferred to somebody who knew about the case. He reassured her that Roger and his brother were, by every indication, most likely on their way to Mexico right now. They had certain contacts there, he said.

"Maybe they were involved in organized crime," commented Bethany's mom. "We hear about all kinds of crime rings and Mob gangs operating all over the place these days. Besides, Roger and his brother would hardly take the chance of coming here, at any rate. The local police would be more familiar with them than the police anywhere else."

I felt almost numb with relief at her words. Of course Bethany's mom was right. It wouldn't make any sense at all for Roger and Will to come here.

"Completely idiotic," I told myself firmly, trying to suppress the tiny bit of doubt that was still nagging inside.

Chapter 3

By the time I arrived at the stable the next day, my fear from the day before appeared more like an unreal dream. Bethany and I had slept a little longer than usual this morning, and the horses greeted us with loud neighing, clearly feeling shamefully neglected.

Núpur looked at me accusingly with his velvety brown eyes as I hurried over to his stall. "Is this how you treat your horse?" he seemed to be saying. "The other horses have long since gotten their hay, while I, poor neglected thing, have to stand here and starve!"

I scratched his forehead and quickly took care of his hunger. He buried his muzzle in the fragrant hay and greedily tore off a big mouthful of it, which he contentedly gobbled down. While he was busy eating, I removed manure and wet straw from his stall, and wheeled it to the dung pile behind the stable.

Afterwards I tethered Núpur in the hallway and started grooming him, giving it my best effort. He totally loved it. I was so absorbed by what I was doing that I jumped at the sound of a voice behind me.

"Hi Rachel, I heard the news yesterday..."

I looked up and saw Martin, the director of the riding school. He came toward me, followed by Erin, one of the girls in the stable. Erin was suspiciously red in the face, something that was not entirely uncommon when Martin was nearby.

During my work, I had actually managed to forget about

Roger, but Martin's words were all it took to wipe the smile off my face.

"Sorry if I reminded you of something you'd rather not talk about," said Martin as he noticed the expression on my face.

I shook my head. "No, it doesn't matter," I said half-heartedly. "It's just that I had managed to stop thinking about Roger for a little while."

I told Martin how I had reacted to the news, and what the police had said.

"It's a relief to hear that he's far away from here at least," said Martin. "Don't you worry about him! You know, most likely the threats he flung at you during the court case were never meant very seriously. I think it's fairly common for such scoundrels to swear revenge upon the person they think is responsible for them being caught. But I don't think many of them actually carry out their threats when they get out."

"Many of them, huh?" I mumbled. Easy enough for Martin to take the threats so lightly. He wasn't there and didn't see the malicious look in Roger's eyes when he said, "You just wait, you little creep. Some day I'll get out and then I'll deal with you..."

I shuddered, looking around for Erin, but she had disappeared while I was talking to Martin. To keep myself from thinking about Roger, I went over to Tanya, who was busy grooming her horse, and asked her, "Would you like to go for a ride with Bethany and me today? We could ride over to the reservoir, or to the woods, or wherever. It's such a beautiful day. I meant to ask Erin too, but I don't know where she went."

"She went into the saddle room. She's fixing a strap on Glonada's bridle, I think," said Tanya. "I'd love to go for a ride. And I'll go in and ask if Erin wants to come, too."

Erin and Tanya are best friends, and they both go to the same Middle school as Bethany and me.

103

Tanya came back and announced that Erin was in. "I was afraid she might want to stay in the stable all day to... help out and stuff," she said meaningfully with a giggle.

I chuckled under my breath, because I was very well aware of what Tanya was hinting at. It had become increasingly apparent during the last few weeks that Erin was in love. She walked around pretty much with her head in the clouds, and did the most ridiculous mistakes every time the object of her infatuation was nearby, which he was quite frequently. Erin could deny it as much as she wanted to, but none of us had any doubt whatsoever that she was head over heels in love with Martin. Personally I didn't get it. Sure, he was good looking and all, but to me he was a grown-up, and I didn't feel anywhere close to being an adult yet. I viewed Martin in the same light as a nice teacher, and couldn't really see him in the role of boyfriend to a fifteen-year-old.

But Erin could, apparently. I only hoped she would get over her infatuation before she made a fool of herself in front of Martin. He was most likely completely unaware of Erin's feelings.

I glanced over at Martin, who was on his way toward the saddle room. Just as he was about to go in, Erin came out carrying Glonada's saddle and bridle. She almost walked right into Martin, stopped, bewildered, and mumbled something I couldn't hear. Martin looked a little confused, but gave her a friendly smile and stepped aside to let her pass. Erin's face turned as red as a lobster, and she hurried over to Glonada and started saddling her up very rapidly.

My first instinct was to tease her about it, but then I decided that doing so wouldn't be very nice of me, or very smart. So I controlled my evil urges and focused on Núpur instead.

When I glanced at Erin a little while later, her face had

returned to its normal color and she was in the process of tightening the girth.

"There's something wrong with these straps," she said irritably.

"Let me see." Tanya rushed to her side and lifted one of the saddle flaps. She scratched her head, and then she apparently saw what was wrong. "Oh, I see what's wrong," she said triumphantly. "The straps have been crossed right here, and they're not supposed to be."

While fixing the straps, she said, "I don't know how you got a simple thing like that messed up, but maybe you had other things on your mind, huh?" She smiled teasingly, and Erin blushed, but didn't say anything.

"Are you guys ready?" I asked impatiently. "At this rate, we'll be retiring before we get out of the stable."

"I'm almost done," said Bethany.

"I just need to take the halter off of Hawk and get his bridle on. That takes four seconds."

Ten minutes later, not four seconds, we were on our way to the reservoir. It was a beautiful day, and the horses seemed very perky and energetic. We let them gallop along the part of the beach that belonged to the riding school, and they seemed to really enjoy themselves. Afterwards we went to a big meadow where they could walk briskly. I totally enjoyed the scenery and Núpur, and I could feel all the way to my toes how lucky I was to have this wonderful horse, and good friends to share my joy of riding with.

"Isn't it strange that hardly any boys like horseback riding?" commented Bethany all of a sudden.

"They have no idea what they're missing," I said. "I guess it's just presumed and generally accepted that boys will only care about sports and video games, besides cars and motorcycles, of course.

"Sounds dreadfully boring to me," commented Tanya. "Actually, video and computer games can be all right sometimes, but it certainly doesn't compare to riding. And I guess there are a few guys who ride. Isn't that so, Erin?"

"Oh, cut it out," said Erin, annoyed.

"Why should I?" asked Tanya, faking innocence. "There's no shame in being in love with Martin, is there? There are worse guys you could have chosen, even if he is a little old for you."

"Don't you think I know perfectly well that he thinks I'm just a kid?" hissed Erin. "But I can't help the way I feel. I turn to jelly as soon as he gets near me, even though I don't want to, and it doesn't make it any better to have you all sniggering and throwing sarcastic hints about it."

"I'm sorry, I won't say another word," said Tanya piously, but I could tell she was struggling to remain serious, and didn't think it would take her long to break that promise.

However, when we got back to the stable from our ride, even Tanya lost all interest in teasing Erin about Martin anymore.

We had started brushing the horses after our ride when Martin showed up and asked if we could do him a big favor.

"Would you guys feed the horses for me tonight, and lock up the stable when you're done?"

"Sure, no problem," I said. "Bethany and I can take care of it together."

"Great!" said Martin with a relieved smile. "I'm going to a dinner party tonight, so I'd better go and clean up."

"Big family dinner?" asked Bethany.

"Well, no... My girlfriend, Lynn, has been bugging me about meeting her parents for some time now, so tonight there's no escaping it." He smiled feebly and actually blushed a little.

I glanced secretively toward Erin, who looked like she had been hit by lightning. Poor Erin! This certainly crushed any hopes she might have had of Martin taking notice of her.

"I didn't even know you had a girlfriend," Tanya blurted out. She almost sounded offended.

"No, why should you?" said Martin surprised. "I don't have any idea if any of you have boyfriends, so we're even there."

After he had left, we concentrated on the horses again. Erin kept brushing and brushing Glonada, even though there wasn't a speck of dust left on her shiny coat. I really felt sorry for her, and wished I could say something to cheer her up. But I was afraid to only make things worse, so I kept my mouth shut. We were an unusually quiet bunch working in the stable that evening. The only thing breaking the silence was Hawk. He was hungry and waiting impatiently to get into his stall so he could eat. And he finally let us know it, loud and clear. Bethany showed mercy on him and let him have the food he so dearly longed for, and silence fell again over the stalls.

I looked at Núpur one last time before we went home. He stood there so peacefully in his stall, munching on a mouthful of hay, and I suddenly felt my whole body filled with an intense love for him.

"See you tomorrow, precious," I said quietly, before I followed Bethany out of the stable. Núpur didn't pay any attention to me. He had more important things to focus on, namely his food.

Chapter 4

The escaped prisoners were mentioned on the news for two days, but as no further information was available, they eventually dropped it altogether. To me it was actually a relief when they stopped talking about it, because I noticed that I got nervous every time Roger's name was mentioned. For the time being I forgot all about Roger and concentrated on enjoying Núpur and the beautiful weather.

Erin wasn't around these days. Tanya told us that she had gone to visit her grandmother, because she hadn't seen her for so long. I suspected that the real reason was Martin, and that Erin wanted to avoid him for a few days, but I didn't say anything about it to Tanya.

One day, while Bethany and I were out riding, the airplane showed up again. I hadn't given it a single thought since the last time we saw it, but I immediately recognized the funny hiccup sound from its engine. This time Bethany and I happened to be inside a grove of trees when the plane appeared. It was flying low, just like the first time.

"Let's wait in here between the trees until the plane is gone," I said quickly to Bethany, as I reined in Núpur. "I don't want that idiot to scare the horses again like he did last time." I leaned forward and patted Núpur lovingly on the neck while talking soothingly to him. It was clear that he recognized the sound too, because he kept flapping his ears nervously. But fortunately he remained calm and showed no signs of panic.

Outside the clump of trees we were hiding under, there was a clearing with an open meadow, and another grove of trees on the other side of it. The plane was now gliding right above us. I looked up.

"Look, Rachel!" said Bethany excitedly. "They're dropping something!"

A few black packages fell from the plane. They hit the ground right by the grove of trees on the other side of the meadow. No sooner had the packages hit the ground, then the plane disappeared with a roar from the engine.

And before either of us had grasped what was happening, two men came running out from the trees on the opposite side, grabbed the packages and disappeared in between the trees again.

"C'mon, let's follow them," I said excitedly.

"Are you out of your mind?" said Bethany in shock. "What if there are drugs in those packages? If so it could be really dangerous to follow those two men. Deliveries like that are worth a fortune to them, and drug dealers don't shy away from anything if somebody gets in their way."

I realized that Bethany was right. It would be madness to put ourselves in that kind of potential danger. We stayed where we were, in between the trees, not knowing what to do, until we heard a car engine starting somewhere in the woods.

"C'mon!" I yelled to Bethany. "They're leaving. At least we can try to get the license number of the car."

I didn't wait to see if Bethany was following. I rode at full speed across the meadow and into the trees on the other side. A little ways ahead of me I glimpsed a dirt road, and steered Núpur toward it.

We emerged from the trees just in time to see the car disappear around a turn in the road. The landscape was so open here; I didn't dare follow the car.

"Did you get the number?" asked Bethany when she caught up with me.

"No, the license plate was so covered in mud that I couldn't make out the numbers," I said.

"All I could tell was that it was an old green Volvo with a spot of reddish brown color on the right side."

"That's not much to go by," sighed Bethany. "But I guess we ought to tell the police regardless, don't you think?"

I nodded. "Yes, I think we should. Of course it's possible that the packages didn't contain drugs, but even so, I'm willing to bet it was something illegal. Why else would they..."

"Ah-choo!"

I turned around, startled. The sound, very much like a sneeze, had come from somewhere behind us.

"Look! – In the thicket over there," said Bethany, shocked.

I looked in the direction she was pointing, and thought I saw the silhouette of a person standing completely still between the tight branches.

"What if it's one of the drug dealers?" said Bethany frightened. "What if he's waiting for us, to get rid of two witnesses?"

"If so, he can just keep waiting," I said as I felt panic well up inside me. "I'm not going to stick around a minute longer."

We took off in a wild gallop, away from the suspicious person in the thicket. I halfway expected to hear the sound of a gunshot, but we managed to get around the bend without anything happening.

The closer we got to the stable, the more unreal the whole thing seemed. Well, not the plane drop, of course. That was real enough. But the man in the bushes – did he exist, or was he just a figment of our imagination? Had we just made a fly into an elephant?

Evidently Bethany had been thinking the same thing, because while we took care of water and food for Núpur and Hawk, she said, "Let's go home and tell my parents what happened, except – not about the man in the thicket. Do you agree? You see, I'm getting more and more unsure that I actually saw somebody."

"Same here," I said. "It'll just sound stupid and hysterical, I think. Let's drop that part of the story."

Bethany's dad called the police, and two officers came to the house and talked to us. They asked all kinds of things, and it was embarrassing to realize just how little we had noticed. We couldn't say much of anything about the plane, other than that it was small and grayish white, and had a hiccup. We couldn't give a good description of the two men who had picked up the packages, and neither did we have the license number of the old Volvo.

"All airplanes are supposed to have some identifying letters on them," said one of the policemen. "Are you sure you didn't notice them?"

Ashamed, Bethany and I looked at each other. We weren't very useful as witnesses, that was clear.

"Oh, now I remember something about one of the men," said Bethany suddenly. "I got the impression he was kind of big and muscular, and I'm pretty sure he had short, dark hair."

The police tried to ask us about the clothes the men had been wearing, but all we could contribute was a rather vague description of one of them maybe wearing a patterned shirt or jacket.

We felt pretty subdued after the policemen left, even though they praised us for having the good sense to not follow the men while they were on foot. It was pretty obvious that the police also believed the men were drug dealers, and that it could have been very dangerous to try to follow them.

"Do you think the men might have seen you?" asked Bethany's dad anxiously after the police had left.

Bethany and I glanced at each other. "I don't think they saw us," I finally said quietly. "And if they did, they would only have gotten a quick glimpse of us and the horses, not enough to recognize us."

"That's good," he said relieved. "I've heard that those kind of people can be very dangerous if they feel threatened."

Bethany and I looked at each other again, and both of us thought about the same thing – the man in the thicket. What if he wasn't just a figment of our imagination? What if he was one of the gangsters? Then he might have had plenty of opportunity to study us carefully, and would be able to recognize us easily.

Chapter 5

Neither Bethany nor I slept very well that night. But in the beautiful sunny weather the next morning, it seemed downright ridiculous that some drug dealer would be hiding behind a bush and spying on us, so we tried to shake off the unpleasant thought and focus on our riding instead.

Erin came back to the stable, and looked very cheerful and happy, so maybe she had actually managed to forget about Martin.

"Do you guys want to go for a ride?" she asked once she was done shoveling Glonada's stall.

"Sure," I said. "But I don't really want to ride in the woods. We had some scary things happen there yesterday."

Then I told Erin and Tanya about the suspicious plane drop and the men who had picked up the packages with illegal drugs.

"At least the police seem to think it was illegal drugs," commented Bethany.

"How exciting!" gushed Tanya delightedly when I had finished telling our story. "I wish I had been there! But I always miss out on the fun, when something finally happens around here!"

"I'd be glad to miss this one," said Bethany. "Man, I was so scared I almost wet my pants!"

While I got Núpur ready for the ride, my mind was totally absorbed by the thought of what had taken place in the woods. I tried to picture the airplane in hopes of remembering more details about it, but it was no use. It remained an anonymous, grayish white thing in my memory. So I moved on to the two men who had picked up the packages. I closed my eyes tight, trying to picture them. There was something about the biggest, more muscular guy that bothered me, but regardless of how much I tried, I couldn't figure out what it was.

Núpur obviously thought I was getting a little too distracted, because he suddenly nudged me with his head and made a loud snort which literally reeked of insult. I put my arms around his neck with a chuckle.

"You poor thing, how neglected you are," I said, scratching him behind the ears.

He thrashed his head impatiently, as if saying, "Haven't we dawdled long enough now? What about that ride? Or did you just put the saddle on my back for the fun of it?"

"All right, all right, we'll go," I laughed as I started leading him through the hallway and out to the farmyard. Over at the riding arena, Martin was trying to teach a group of students how to do the running walk, or tolt, as it's called. As far as I could tell, only a couple of them were anywhere close to getting it right.

Martin turned around and waved to us as we rode past them. I threw a quick glance at Erin, but she looked completely normal and relaxed. She didn't even blush, so maybe a few days away from the stable actually *had* cured her of the 'Martin bug'.

We had decided to ride up on the hill, where the landscape was open and the ground was nice and level, making it a great place for galloping.

We chatted as we rode uphill, and Bethany asked Erin if she had a good time at her grandma's.

"I had a great time," said Erin. "My grandmother is pretty cool, actually. You know what? She even took me to a rock concert! Wasn't that nice of her? It was a lot of fun too. The only drawback was that we had to take a long, boring bus ride to and from. But the trip home went pretty fast actually, because I happened to see a boy from school on the bus, and we started talking. His name's Logan and he's in 8th grade at our school.

"Oh, yeah, I know who he is," I burst out. "Tall and thin, with dark, curly hair, right? Very cute."

"And very nice," nodded Erin.

"Will you be seeing him again?" Bethany wanted to know.

Erin blushed. "Well, he asked if I would go to a movie with him," she said, trying to sound casual.

"And judging by the color of your face, I'd say you did not decline," said Tanya.

Erin stuck her tongue out at her friend, but then she laughed.

I looked at her, happy that she had somebody other than Martin to think about. Logan was a nice guy, no doubt about that. I had actually been secretly in love with him myself a year ago. But it never turned into anything other than a secret, and after a few weeks my infatuation went away by itself.

I looked at Núpur who moved along smoothly and rhythmically under me. Boys are okay, I thought, but they still don't measure up to horses. I bent forward and patted Núpur on the neck. "You're much better than any boy, right?" I said to him. Núpur didn't answer, but I doubt he would disagree with my notion that he was the best thing in the world.

"Is there anything in the world better than this?" gushed Bethany when we pulled up the horses after a vigorous gallop.

"If there is, it would be a nice, cold drink," said Tanya. "I'm parched."

"There's a brook over there, if you want some fresh water," I said, pointing.

We dismounted by some big rocks, and Tanya ran toward the brook. "Ah, that was delicious," she said when she came back.

"Could one of you look after Hawk for me?" asked Bethany. "I must have drunk a little too much orange juice for breakfast, so I'll have to go and find a bush somewhere."

"Why don't you just go behind those rocks over there?" suggested Tanya and pointed.

Bethany left. But when she got to the rocks, she suddenly stopped and turned toward us.

"Come over here – quick!" she shouted, sounding shocked. "Somebody's lying in the grass!"

With the horses in tow, we hurried over to her. She had knelt down next to a man. He was lying on his stomach in the grass, completely still. Bethany reached out her hand and touched him.

"Ugh! He's... he's as cold as ice," she said quietly as she withdrew her hand.

"I checked for a pulse, but there wasn't any!"

"Do you mean – he's dead?" I asked in disbelief.

Bethany nodded. Her face had turned completely white, and I noticed that her hands were shaking. "I think he's been dead for some time," she said.

We stood there in a half-circle, totally at a loss, just staring. Finally Tanya collected herself and said in a shaky voice, "What are we going to do? Try to take him with us to the ranch?"

Bethany thought about it, and then shook her head firmly. "No, we'd better not touch him," she said, "We don't know what happened to him."

I felt a pang of relief at her words. Just the thought of touching a dead man made me feel sick. Quickly, I turned away from the motionless body.

"I suggest we ride back and get some help," said Erin resolutely. "Rachel, you and Bethany can ride down to Martin and tell him, and Tanya and I can stay here and wait."

I was glad to do as she said. Relieved, I swung myself into Núpur's saddle, and shortly after Bethany and I rode as fast as we could down the hill toward the riding school.

Martin was shocked to hear what we had found, but reacted quickly and called the police. They responded surprisingly fast, and Bethany and I showed them the way to the place where Tanya and Erin were waiting.

The police thanked us for the help and told us all to go back to the stable. We were glad about that.

The police also said they wanted to talk to us later, so while we waited for them to come back, we stayed in the farmyard grooming the horses, and trying to think about something other than the horrible discovery we had made. Of course, we weren't able to.

"What do you think he died of?" asked Tanya after we ran out of idle chitchat.

"I have no idea. A heart attack, maybe?" I suggested feebly. That seemed like something I had heard a lot of men die from.

"Maybe he fell and was killed in the fall," said Erin.

"I doubt it. There wasn't a drop of blood anywhere that I could see," commented Tanya. "If he had hit his head against one of the rocks – wouldn't there be blood there?"

We discussed the issue back and forth, without getting any wiser, and it seemed like an eternity before the police finally showed up.

It was a young policeman who approached us, and we immediately gathered around the poor guy, pelting him with all kinds of questions.

He held up his hand in an attempt to ward off the onslaught. "Please, ladies, let's take one thing at a time," he begged. "First of all, let me thank you all for having the good sense to not disturb the scene."

"Why would it matter?" asked Bethany. "I mean, the guy was dead already, wasn't he?"

The policeman nodded. "Oh yes, definitely. But he didn't die a natural death."

"What?" I gasped. "Do you mean he was murdered?"

The police officer hesitated, then said slowly, "I might as well tell you now, because it'll be on the news tonight regardless. The man was shot."

"But couldn't he have done it himself?" asked Tanya. "That happens quite a bit, doesn't it?"

The policeman shook his head determinedly. "If it was a suicide, the gun would have still been there," he said. "There was no gun nearby."

"But how could he have been shot?" objected Bethany. "There was no blood!"

"We can't say for sure until after the autopsy," said the policeman, "but everything points at him being shot somewhere else, and then dumped at the site in the hills."

"I'm sure glad we didn't try to move him," said Erin in a feeble voice. "If we had turned him over, we would probably have seen the shot wound – ugh! I can't stand to even think about it."

I felt about as sick as Erin did, but I still had an even bigger shock in store. It came when Bethany asked, "Do you know who the bo... uh... the dead man is?"

The police officer nodded. "He was reported missing a few days ago, along with his brother. His name was Will Soto.

Chapter 6

"Rachel! Rachel, can you hear me?"

I was lying on the ground, but didn't understand how I got there. Wasn't I standing up just a second ago? I sat up, feeling totally confused. Above me, four faces appeared in a hazy fog, and a man's voice said quietly, "Don't try to get up yet. You just fainted."

It felt like the ground was moving, and I had no desire to stand up. So I obeyed and remained sitting, while listening to the conversation flying back and forth above my head. I heard Bethany telling the policeman why Will Soto's name had given me such a shock.

"This probably means that Roger Soto is also in the vicinity," Bethany said.

I didn't catch what the policeman said, but only a few minutes later, Bethany and I sat in his car on our way back to Bethany's house. I felt shaky, but was otherwise all right now. Bethany's dad was home, and he and the police officer stayed in the living room and talked for quite a while. Bethany and I had been told to go out on the back porch, where we sat in silence. We tried to listen in on the conversation taking place inside, but the voices were so muffled, we couldn't make out any words.

After a while the police officer took off, and Bethany's dad came out and joined us on the porch.

"I don't like this at all," he said as he sat down next to us. "Murder, right here, in our own neighborhood. And one of the scoundrels is still out there, probably desperate and dangerous."

"Do the police think it was Roger who shot Will? I asked with big, surprised eyes.

"The police officer didn't say anything about that, but who else would it be? The two of them ran away together."

"But why would Roger do a thing like that?" I shook my head, befuddled.

Bethany's dad shrugged his shoulders. "Who knows?" he said. "Maybe they were fighting about something. Or maybe Will got cold feet and wanted to give himself up to the police? We probably won't find out until they arrest Roger."

"But what if they don't catch him?" I said with a shudder. "What if he comes after me and carries out his threats?"

"That's exactly what I wanted to talk to the police about, and they've promised to keep our house under surveillance, just in case Roger is sneaking around nearby. But they're leaning more toward the theory that he has other things to worry about right now. If he was the one who killed Will, he'll probably try to put as much distance between himself and this place as possible, as soon as possible."

I nodded somewhat reluctantly. It sounded completely logical, but I couldn't manage to shake the feeling that Roger was somewhere close by. I thought I could almost feel his evil, glaring eyes on my neck. The feeling was so strong that I involuntarily turned my head to look. Nobody was there, of course. I let my eyes glide across the yard and toward the bushes surrounding it. Suddenly I gave a start. Over there, in the hedge, wasn't that an extra dark shadow in there? I squinted my eyes. No, it must have been my imagination. I turned resolutely toward the table again. I'd better not let my imagination get out of control. Of course Roger wasn't sitting in the hedge spying on me.

"... and call them right away."

"What?" I asked, confused, looking at Bethany's dad.

"I was saying I'd better go and call your parents right away, and tell them what happened."

"Oh no, please don't!" I begged. "Please don't tell them! If Mom hears there's the slightest chance that Roger might be nearby, she'll come right home instantly. And if she does, their vacation, the seminar and everything will be completely ruined for them."

"But..." started Bethany's dad.

"Dad, didn't you say yourself that Roger's probably not around here anymore?" interrupted Bethany. "Then what's the point of scaring Rachel's parents? Besides, Rachel's staying here with us, so that ought to be safe enough, don't you think?"

"We promise we won't ride in the woods or anything on our own," I added. "Pretty please...?"

We continued to discuss the issue for a while, and Bethany's dad finally gave in.

"But you'd better keep all your promises, do you hear me?" he said with urgency. "If you so much as poke a horse's nose into the woods, or ride off to some out-of-the-way place without at least four or five others accompanying you, I will call Rachel's parents on the spot, is that clear?"

"Crystal clear!" said Bethany, and I nodded. Right now I didn't feel much like riding out alone anyway.

"The plane drop!" exclaimed Bethany all of a sudden. "Do you think Roger and Will may have been involved in that drug delivery thing?"

And suddenly a light came on in my head. "It was Roger and Will we saw in the woods that day!" I shouted triumphantly. "I thought there was something familiar about one of those men! I recognized the shape of the back of his head. It was Roger, I'm sure of it!"

Bethany's dad didn't look very convinced, but he still went inside and called the police. When he came back out, he told us that the police apparently had already suspected the same thing, but he hadn't managed to find out anything more than that.

During dinner, Martin came by with our bicycles, which we had left behind at the riding school.

"I thought you might need them," he said. "And since I had to go into town anyway, I figured I might as well take them along in the truck."

Before Martin left again, he said that Núpur and Hawk were in the small pasture, and that it was a good idea to put them in the stable for the night, sooner rather than later. "There's an unusual amount of flies out in the pasture tonight, so the horses will definitely be happy to get away from those pesky little things."

At first, Bethany's dad didn't want us to ride our bikes to the stable, but Bethany said, "C'mon, Dad, the bike path is right next to a busy highway. Nobody can attack us there without at least ten witnesses."

So he reluctantly agreed to let us go. While we biked toward the riding school, we talked about all the scary things that had happened in such a short period of time. Bethany had an idea about why Will had been killed.

"Do you remember the first time we saw that plane?" she asked.

I nodded.

"I doubt that Roger and Will were around here at that time. That was right after they ran away. Do you know what I think? I think that the original plane drop was thwarted because we showed up in the meadow that time. The drug delivery was actually meant for someone else, but somehow Roger and

Will got wind of it and snatched the delivery when it came the second time."

"But what about the people who were supposed to get it then? Why didn't they show up?" I objected.

"I think they did show up. But Roger and Will were faster. Remember the person who was hiding in the bushes, watching as the Volvo drove away? I think the package was meant for him. And if we hadn't showed up, he might just have shot both Roger and Will right there and then. But he probably heard the thumping of hooves as we approached, and had to hide. So instead he was forced to wait for another opportunity to get the drugs back from them. I bet he was the one who shot Will!"

"I think you've seen too many detective shows," I said. "But I have to admit that your idea doesn't sound too unreasonable, even though it could just as easily have been Roger who shot him. He and Will might have been fighting over the booty or something, like your dad said. I just don't understand how Roger and Will found out about the plane drop, if the goods weren't intended for them."

Bethany didn't have a good explanation for that. I thought that most likely Roger and Will were the drug dealers, and that Roger had shot Will for some reason or other – maybe because he wanted the money all for himself. I shuddered. Regardless of how many times I tried to remind myself that Roger definitely would be far away by now, I couldn't quite believe it. I had this creepy feeling that he was somewhere nearby, waiting – and watching me...

Chapter 7

"I bet Núpur and Hawk will be glad to get into the stable," said Bethany while we walked toward the small pasture. "This has to be the biggest fly plague ever. Martin was right, the air is absolutely thick with these pesky little things."

Hawk was standing peacefully underneath a tree, lazily fanning away flies with his tail. But Núpur was nowhere to be seen.

"That's strange," I said. "Maybe Martin got back from town and took him inside already."

"Maybe the flies were bothering him too much," suggested Bethany.

But when we came into the stable, we saw right away that Núpur's stall was empty. Where in the world was Núpur? Could Martin have lent him to somebody without asking me first?

I heard a car driving up and ran outside. It was Martin arriving. He parked the car behind the stable and came walking around the corner and into the farmyard, looking totally carefree. But the cheerful smile on his face disappeared when I asked him where he had put Núpur.

"What do you mean, where did I put him? Isn't he out in the pasture?" he said, confused. "He was out there, grazing peacefully when I left and went into town."

He came with us to the pasture to see for himself and make doubly sure that our eyesight hadn't suddenly failed us. But there was no Núpur out there, that much was certain.

"Maybe he found a hole in the fence and slipped outside for a little adventure," suggested Bethany.

"That could be what happened, I guess," nodded Martin. "Let's just hope he hasn't wandered off toward the highway. If we find the hole in the fence, it might point us in his direction."

We followed the fence from the gate and all the way around, but saw no sign of a hole anywhere.

"Are you sure the gate was closed when you arrived?" Martin asked.

"A hundred percent sure," I said firmly.

"Then I'm afraid there's only one explanation left," said Martin gravely. "Somebody must have taken Núpur."

"What?" I was dumbfounded as I stared at him. The idea that Núpur might have been stolen had never occurred to me. I'd only worried about whether he might be wandering around near the highway. Now I suddenly felt sick with worry. Who could possibly have been mean enough to steal my horse, and where was he now?

Martin thought that we should bike around the area to look for Núpur, just in case. So for the next two hours or more, we peddled around on every road and trail in the vicinity, but didn't see a single sign of Núpur. By the time we got back to the riding school, I was on the verge of tears. While we had been gone, Martin had spoken to the others who had been in the stable while he was in town, and one of the girls told him that she had seen a man walking by the pasture. Unfortunately she couldn't remember what he looked like, nor had she noticed whether he went into the pasture or not.

"I'll go and call the police," said Martin. "They'll probably be able to track him down."

He didn't really sound very optimistic, and I got a sickening feeling that I would never see Núpur again.

Bethany tried to comfort me, but I got more and more upset by the minute.

"What if he's been taken away in a horse trailer?" I said. "The thieves could be miles from here by now, and how will the police manage to track him down then?"

Martin came back and said that the police had asked for a photo of Núpur, to make it easier for them to recognize him in case they came across something suspicious.

I biked home as fast as I could to get a picture. Bethany offered to come with me, but I told her it wasn't necessary.

"It's rush hour traffic, and the roads are packed with cars. I'll be safe for such a short distance. You just stay here and take care of Hawk."

Bethany agreed, and I flew off toward home. My mind was spinning with thoughts of what might have happened to Núpur. I couldn't understand why anybody would steal my horse. Why mine? Of course he was the most fantastic horse in the world as far as I was concerned, but I knew perfectly well that some of the other Icelandic horses in the stable were worth a lot more than he – for several reasons. For instance, most of them were good tolting horses.

Could it be that the thieves had taken the wrong horse? Or was it possible that... No – the idea that Roger had anything to do with this was a little too far-fetched. What would he do with a horse? He couldn't exactly run from the police on horseback.

As I parked my bike in the driveway at home, I regretted not having asked Bethany to come with me after all. The house seemed so dark and foreboding, and I suddenly felt reluctant to go inside. But I had to, if I was going to get that picture of Núpur for the police.

"Get a grip on yourself, and quit being such a wimp!" I told myself sternly. "It's broad daylight, and you have nothing to be afraid of. Two minutes inside, and you'll be all done and on your way back again."

I unlocked the door and walked slowly into the entrance. Now, where did I put that envelope of photos with the latest pictures of Núpur? Oh, yes, on the bookshelf, I thought. I went into the living room and over to the bookshelf. Sure enough, I immediately saw the photos on the bottom shelf.

"So! You finally came," said a voice behind me.

I didn't need to turn around to know whose voice it was, but my body spun around anyway, like a marionette being pulled by strings. I was so scared, I couldn't even scream.

"Happy to see me?" asked Roger, with a malicious twinkle in his eyes.

I couldn't make a sound, just tottered unsteadily to the nearest chair for support.

"Why did you come here?" I finally said in a croaky voice.

Roger snickered. "Well, I thought it was a practical thing to do," he said lightly. "I found out that the house was empty at the moment, and I needed a new hideout – fast."

The smile left his face. For a moment he almost looked scared, but then the malicious expression came back.

"Missing a horse, are you?" he asked.

I gasped out loud. So my suspicions were right!

"Why did you steal Núpur? What do you want with a horse?"

"You could say it's my insurance," said Roger.

"Insurance? What do you mean?"

"If you want to see your horse again, alive, you won't tell a soul that I'm hiding here. Do you understand?"

He bent down over me with a threatening expression on his face.

"You... you can't hide here," I said frantically. "Mom and Dad are coming home tomorrow."

"Don't mess around with me!" hissed Roger and grabbed my shoulder. He grabbed me hard enough to make it hurt. "I heard every word you guys said out there on your friend's back porch, so I know exactly how long they'll be gone."

So it hadn't been a figment of my imagination after all! Somebody had been in the bushes, listening, exactly as I had felt. Why didn't I say something right then and there? If I had, maybe Roger would have been arrested already. But there was no point in thinking about that now.

"I don't understand why you had to steal Núpur and let me know that you were here at all," I said, confused. "Why didn't you just hide upstairs, and nobody would have found out?"

"I would have, except that I need you. I need you to do something for me. And the horse is my guaranty that you will do exactly as I say."

"What do you want me to do?" I whispered in fear.

"Two things," said Roger. "First of all, you are not to say a word to anyone about me being here, and secondly, you need to go and get a very important message for me."

"Where am I going?"

"I'll tell you tomorrow. I have the whole escape route worked out. I'm just waiting for my transportation to be confirmed. My contact will have everything ready for me tomorrow, and I'm supposed to meet him then. But with the current situation being what it is, I can't be seen near his house. So I need you to meet him instead."

"You don't dare go outside because the police are after you?" I asked hesitantly.

"Hah! The police?" Roger snorted contemptuously. "If the police were my only worry, I'd have no problems. It's not much of a challenge to fool those idiots."

"Is it because of the drugs?"

Roger nodded dismally. "We thought we had everything under control," he said, "but then things went haywire."

"And then Will got killed. Did you shoot him?"

I could tell by the expression on Roger's face that he didn't like my question, but he finally said in a brusque voice, "No, of course not. Why would I shoot my own brother?"

I didn't answer, but I thought to myself that somebody who robs his own wife and then tries to blame it on her ex-husband, probably doesn't shy away from anything.

I looked Roger in the eyes. Was he telling the truth? I wondered. It was impossible to say. But regardless of whether he was the killer or not, he looked desperate enough that he would probably not hesitate to kill a horse if I made trouble for him.

"I'll do anything you say," I promised. "Just don't hurt Núpur, please."

Roger squinted his eyes while he looked at me, as if he wasn't sure that I meant what I said. But then he nodded. "It's a deal. And don't think it will do any good to go looking for your horse. He's hidden in a remote, isolated place, where nobody would think to look."

"Did you shut Núpur inside somewhere without food?" I asked in horror.

He shook his head impatiently.

"I'm not a complete idiot! The horse has plenty of food and water, don't worry about that. You just make sure you do exactly as I say, and then everything will be fine. But if you don't, you'll definitely have something to worry about, I promise you that!"

I believed him.

Chapter 8

It wasn't easy to act as if nothing had happened when I got back to the riding school. Roger had ordered me to stop by the house again the next day.

"You pick up the mail every afternoon, right?" he said, nodding toward the pile of letters and newspapers that were lying on the hallway table.

I couldn't very well deny that. "Yes, I usually put the mail inside before Bethany and I go back to her place for dinner."

"Well, make sure you come alone tomorrow," he said before I left. "Or else you can kiss your horse goodbye!"

Bethany and Martin were waiting for me outside the stable. I gave the picture of Núpur to Martin, who nodded approvingly. "This is an excellent photo. If the police come across the thieves, they shouldn't have any problem identifying Núpur based on this."

I didn't say anything, and Bethany threw me a searching glance . "Is something wrong? You look different," she said.

I turned away from her. "Of course something's wrong," I said stiffly. "My horse was stolen!"

"But hopefully you'll have it back soon," said Martin in a vain attempt at cheering me up. "I'll take this photo to the police right away, and then it's just a matter of waiting for good news."

"As if the police are going to bother looking for a horse," I mumbled after Martin had left. Actually, I hoped I was right, because I felt guilty about having the police waste time looking for Núpur, when I knew they would be looking in vain. Roger had said that Núpur was hidden in a deserted place where nobody would think to look for him.

"If the police haven't found him by tomorrow morning, we can start looking for him as well," suggested Bethany. "What if we're totally on the wrong track and he wasn't stolen at all? What if he somehow managed to get out in a way we haven't thought of yet? Then he might still be wandering around this area."

I nodded without any enthusiasm and noticed Bethany searching my face.

I had a terrible night. One nightmare after the other interfered with my sleep. One moment I was being followed by some crazy murderer who said he was out to get me, and the next moment I was climbing up a steep mountain, screaming and hollering at Roger, who was standing at the top, ready to push Núpur over a cliff. I was glad when morning finally came and I could get up. We called the police, but they had no news for us.

Bethany and I made a big detour on our bikes when we rode to the riding school, in order to look for Núpur. That is, Bethany looked for him. I just pretended to. I knew he wasn't wandering around the neighborhood, but I couldn't very well refuse to look for him, because then Bethany would definitely get suspicious.

The night before, she had tried to question me about what was really bothering me, because she believed it was more than just Núpur being gone. But I evaded her questions, and said I was tired and wanted to go to bed.

Martin was waiting for us when we biked into the farmyard.

"Hi!" he said. "Any news?"

We both shook our heads.

131

"None here either," Martin said regretfully. "But I have an idea."

I looked at him questioningly.

"Rachel, there's a horse available that you can borrow this morning. Then you and Bethany can ride back and forth across the meadows and fields and look for Núpur. We can't totally ignore the possibility that he's wandering about on his own, even if it's not very likely. Tanya and Erin have already gone out for a ride, and they promised to keep an eye out for Núpur. Since they're going up in the hills, I suggest you two go somewhere else."

A little while later, Bethany and I were on our way. It felt strange to ride a horse other than Núpur again. Joker, the horse I was borrowing, had choppier and more uneven movements than what I was used to, and he had an annoying habit of tossing his head as he walked. But overall, he was a pretty good riding horse, I guess. He just wasn't Núpur! I wondered if I would ever see my horse again. What guaranty did I have that Roger would keep his promise? He had certainly been lying big time while he lived with my mom, so how could I trust him now?

But I knew I didn't have any choice. I couldn't risk anything else. If I got in the way of Roger's plans, Núpur would be in trouble, I didn't doubt that for a second. It made me sick just to think about it, and the nightmare where Núpur was pushed over a cliff came back to haunt me.

"Hey, are you in a trance or something?" Bethany's voice interrupted my gloomy thoughts. "You won't find the horse by sitting there all hunched up and staring at the ground."

I lifted my head with a jerk and saw that we were on a charming little country road going past some ranches.

"Sorry," I mumbled. "I was thinking about Núpur."

"Well, I think it's something else, other than Núpur, that's bothering you," said Bethany.

132

"Won't you please tell me what it is? I thought we were best friends and could tell each other everything," she continued when I didn't answer. "Don't you trust me?"

"Of course I trust you," I said quickly.

"Well, then prove it!" Bethany pressed.

And suddenly I couldn't help myself; I blurted out the whole story, only interrupted by various exclamations from Bethany. She was really shocked to hear the details of my involuntary meeting with Roger and how he had threatened me.

"That... that jerk!" she said after I was done. "You poor thing, no wonder you didn't look interested in looking for Núpur along roads and fields. So, we should instead be looking in some deserted place where nobody usually goes?"

I nodded. "At least that's what he said."

"If we could just find out where he's hiding Núpur, he wouldn't have any hold on you anymore, and then we could go straight to the police," said Bethany eagerly.

I looked around dismally. "The problem is, there are so many mountains and hidden-away canyons around here. Where in the world would we start looking?

Later, when we got back to the riding school at mid-day, we were both pretty sweaty and discouraged. We had tried riding up some of the mountains and through various small canyons, but had seen no trace of a horse. It eventually dawned on us just how impossible this search was. Two people simply could not cover as large an area as the one we were dealing with.

Bethany thought we should let Martin, Tanya and Erin in on the truth, so that we would at least have five people searching, but I refused. I simply didn't dare risk it. What if Roger's friend happened to find out that we were searching the backcountry for Núpur? If so, Roger might get so furious that he threw all caution to the wind and went off to make good on his threats.

We unsaddled and groomed the horses, and then headed back to Bethany's house. After we ate, we went up to Bethany's room and sat down for a while, hoping for some bright idea to come that might lead us to Núpur. I didn't really have much hope of anything useful coming out of it, though, because I hadn't thought of anything else all day, and it hadn't helped a bit.

The more we pondered and talked about the problem, the more discouraged and depressed I got. There just didn't seem to be any hope of finding Núpur on our own.

But suddenly Bethany jumped up, shouting, "I've got it! I have a great idea!"

I looked at her doubtfully.

"It suddenly occurred to me that it's actually kind of strange for Roger to be so eager to tell you that Núpur is hidden in a remote, isolated place," she said.

"What's so strange about it?" I asked. "I guess he just wanted to make sure I don't start looking for Núpur."

"Exactly!" said Bethany.

I stared at her. Had she lost her mind completely?

"What if he said it only to make you *think* that Núpur is far away?" continued Bethany before I could say anything. "After all, can you really picture Roger way up in the mountains, dragging along a reluctant horse?"

I hadn't even thought about that. But now that Bethany mentioned it, it didn't make any sense at all for Roger to risk going way into the backcountry, especially if it was true that a bunch of dangerous gangsters were after him too.

"Do you remember that Agatha Christie book you borrowed from me a few weeks ago?" asked Bethany.

"The ABC Murders, you mean?" I didn't understand what

134

Bethany was getting at. What on earth did a mystery book have to do with a lost horse?

"Yes, that one. In that book, the detective says, after he solves the case, 'What is the easiest place to hide a murder? In a series of murders!' So what I'm thinking is, the same thing is true for horses!"

I finally saw where she was going. "What's the easiest place to hide a horse? Among a whole bunch of other horses, of course! Bethany, you're a genius!"

"May I have that in writing please?" chuckled Bethany. Then she got serious. "But remember, it's just an idea," she said. "You know, we *could* be totally wrong."

"Regardless, it's the best idea I've heard so far," I said, jumping out of my chair. "What are we waiting for?"

Chapter 9

Martin didn't have a chance when Bethany started talking him into letting us borrow Joker again. She told him we had received an anonymous tip about where we might find Núpur.

Martin thought we should report it to the police, but Bethany managed to avert this.

"I think we should check it out by ourselves first," she said. "What if the anonymous tip is just a stupid prank? If so, it would be a little embarrassing to arrive with police cars and sirens and the whole works!"

"Oh, I doubt they would use sirens," commented Martin, but he agreed to let us have Joker.

"Am I good, or what?" gloated Bethany after we had saddled up the horses and were ready to take off.

However, her gloating stopped abruptly when Martin suddenly shouted to us, "If you actually do come back with Núpur, I want the whole story about how you found out where he is, because I don't buy that nonsense about an anonymous tip, just so you know!"

"Gee! That man is a little too quick for me," grumbled Bethany as she shook her head. "And here I thought I'd been so convincing."

We knew of four large pastures that had a lot of horses in them, and we visited them one by one. In the beginning I was super optimistic, but by the time we had thoroughly examined three of the pastures without finding Núpur, my optimism had taken a serious dive. We were just about to move on to the last pasture, when suddenly a horse who apparently had been lying down behind a bush, got up and lazily shook its head, making its mane flutter.

"Núpur!" I shouted, so loudly that poor Joker startled underneath me. I patted him calmingly on the neck before I quickly slid down on the ground. My legs were shaking as I climbed the fence and ran toward the beautiful Buckskin Icelandic horse.

"What if it isn't him after all?" I thought. "Núpur!" I called hesitantly. He turned his head instantly and neighed in recognition. Two seconds later I had my arms around his neck, while tears of happiness trickled into his mane. I was so happy I didn't know what to do. Eventually I led Núpur with me to the fence and fastened the lead rope on him, which we had brought just in case. Bethany looked just as happy as I was, even though she shook her head in faked resignation at my repeated hugging of Núpur.

"If you're done being all mushy, maybe we could figure out what we're going to do now," she said laughingly.

"Do?" I looked uncomprehendingly at her. "We're going to take Núpur home, of course!"

"Yes, of course we are," nodded Bethany. "But maybe we ought to go to the nearest farm first and explain the situation – at least part of it. And then call the police so they can go straight to your house and arrest Roger."

The farmer lady we talked to was very helpful, and a little while later we were riding slowly and cheerfully back home, with Núpur on a tether behind us. I kept turning around repeatedly just to make sure that he was still with us. When we finally turned into the farmyard outside the stable Martin was there, greeting us with a big smile on his face. "I saw you way down the road," he said. "Good job, girls! I can't tell you how happy I am to see that you found him. And now I want the whole truth and nothing but the truth. How did you find Núpur, and why did you have to be so darned secretive about everything?"

We both started talking simultaneously as we unsaddled the horses.

Martin's face turned dark with anger when I mentioned Roger's name. Since Martin had also been a suspect for a short while after the robbery, he had no warm feelings toward Roger.

"So now, we'll just have to wait until the police have Roger safely under lock and key," said Bethany cheerfully. "I expect the police will call my parents, and hopefully they'll have good news for us by the time we get home."

"Are you guys planning to come back here after dinner?" asked Martin.

"Yes, we are. Why?" I asked.

"Well, I'm going out tonight, and I wondered if you could please do a final check on the horses for the night. I already asked Tanya and Erin, but Tanya has a family dinner tonight and Erin's going to the movies with somebody."

Bethany and I looked knowingly at each other.

"Aha, I bet the somebody's name is Logan," I said. "And sure, we'll see to the horses and lock up the stable – no problem."

"So, another dinner party, is it?" giggled Bethany.

Martin blushed. "No, not a dinner party exactly, but Lynn and I are going out to that new Italian restaurant that opened last week."

"Sounds like fun," I said distractedly. I was getting antsy to go home to Bethany's house and hear news about Roger.

I wish I'd been there to see him when the police barged in, I thought, feeling a little vindictive. I bet they wiped the smirk off his face! And I hope they put him in jail for many, many years!

Chapter 10

By the time I got back to the stable a couple of hours later, however, I knew that the police had not wiped any smirks off of Roger's face at all. Our house had been empty, and the only proof that Roger had been there was a note for me, which he had left on the kitchen table. The note read:

Your horse is in a pasture south of town. Go and find him yourself!

The police assumed that Roger's contact had been able to arrange transport sooner than expected and had found a way to notify Roger.

I thought it sounded a little strange, because according to what Roger said, nobody else knew where he was hiding. But I figured he must have gotten impatient and had taken the chance of going to see his friend after all.

Frankly, I was a little impressed that Roger had bothered to leave me a note telling me where Núpur was. He could easily have left without bothering. Maybe he wasn't so evil after all? But then I remembered the mean, glaring look on his face when he threatened to kill Núpur, and decided that he certainly wasn't worth my sympathy.

"At least he didn't get to hurt you, Núpur," I said and stroked my horse across his silky, soft muzzle. Núpur flapped his ears and snorted contentedly. He was clearly enjoying all the attention. Since Bethany and I had gotten back to the stable, I had practically glued myself to him. It felt so wonderful to have him back; I spent a long time brushing him just so I could feel his warm, thick coat under my fingers. But most of the time I paced back and forth just chatting with him, and also with Bethany, who was fussing over Hawk.

"Do you think they'll eventually catch Roger?" she asked, slipping a little treat to Hawk. He gobbled it up eagerly and sniffed her hand in hopes of finding more.

"You're such a glutton," she laughed. "But you can't have any more now. You'll be getting your hay soon, and then it's time to go to sleep."

"To be honest, I don't care if Roger is caught or not," I said after a moment's thought. "What matters is that I won't have to see him again for the rest of my life. Whether he's in jail or running away to Mexico, it doesn't make much difference to me."

"Well, I don't agree," objected Bethany. "I think it would be too bad if he gets away with a big batch of drugs. Think about all the people who ruin their lives because of vermin like him, who make a profit on selling that disgusting poison. They even sell it to kids, you know!"

"You're right, of course," I said. "I didn't think about that. I was only focused on my own delight in the fact that the sleazebag is out of my life for good. Anyhow, I don't really think the police have much chance of catching him now. It sounded to me as if he had a very carefully planned escape route.

Chapter 11

Two days later, Roger and everything that had happened seemed like a distant, bad dream. I turned out to be right in my prediction that the police wouldn't catch him, so I assumed his escape had gone as planned.

Bethany, Tanya, Erin and I went on rides together, and we kept teasing Erin, who was always in such a hurry these days, eager to finish up and go home for the night.

"I guess this time the allure's a two-legged stallion," joked Tanya as Erin, for the second day in a row, got on her bike and disappeared down the road like a rocket.

"Evidently she's not the only one who has plans for the evening," I giggled, pointing at the door where Martin just appeared. "He looks like he wants to ask us something, but is afraid to."

"Poor guy, let's make it easy for him," suggested Bethany and turned to Martin, "Sure, Martin – we'll see to the horses and lock up the stable. No problem!"

At first Martin looked a little taken aback, but then he smiled. "Wow! A stable full of telepaths – how about that!" he said cheerfully. "So all I need to do is stand in the doorway from now on? I don't even have to ask anymore?" We all laughed.

"Ahh – the wonder of young love!" exclaimed Bethany dramatically after Martin had left. "I guess it's up to us sensible grown-ups to take care of mundane chores."

I laughed. "This is one chore I actually don't mind," I said and ruffled Núpur's mane. He sniffed eagerly at my pockets, as if he knew that I had a couple of carrot pieces hidden away for him. I had to push his muzzle away to even get the treats out of my pocket, making him snort with insult. But the insult quickly gave way to contented munching.

"All right, I'll be going now," shouted Tanya a little while later. "See you guys tomorrow!"

On her way out, she collided with Sidney, one of the younger girls at the riding school. "Hi!" said Sidney, out of breath. "Do you know where Martin is?"

"Martin went home already," said Tanya. "He had an important date with his beloved, or something like that. Why?"

"I was supposed to give him a message from my dad," said Sidney. "It's about a horse that Martin wanted to look at. Dad said he should call the owner as soon as possible."

"Well, you can always go to Martin's house and give him the message. Do you know where he lives?" asked Tanya.

Sidney shook her head. "I have no idea," she said. "But the number he's supposed to call is written on this note," she added. "Couldn't I just leave it here in the stable for him? I was supposed to give it to him when I had my lesson this afternoon, but I forgot, and now I have to hurry – I was supposed to be home an hour ago. My mom's going to kill me!"

With that, she rushed out the door, with Tanya right behind her. Bethany and I were left standing there with the note. I was just about to pin it to the stable message board when Bethany said, "You know what? I think I'll bike over to Martin's house with the note right away. It sounded like it might be something urgent, and if Sidney was supposed to give it to him this afternoon..."

"But what if Martin left already?" I asked.

142

"Then I'll just tape the note to his door and write a quick explanation of what it's about. He can decide for himself if he wants to call this person later tonight."

"Do you want me to come with you?" I asked.

Bethany shook her head. "No, you don't have to," she said, then added teasingly, "You just stay here and cuddle Núpur a little more."

She laughed and ducked just in time to miss the wad of hay I threw at her as she went toward the door.

I turned to Núpur. "She's rude, isn't she?" I said as I ruffled his mane. "As if there's anything wrong with me being delighted to have you back!" Núpur looked at me with his beautiful, dark eyes, and I got a lump in my throat from the sheer joy of having him back with me, all hale and hearty.

Moments later I heard the door being opened. Was Bethany back already? No, she couldn't be, she'd just left on her bike. It must be Tanya who had forgotten something. I turned around, and froze on the spot. It couldn't be true; this couldn't be happening!

But it was true. Roger was standing in the doorway, staring at me. He looked completely mad, and suddenly he came running toward me.

He's come to kill me, was the thought that flashed through my mind. *He found out that I tattled about where he was staying*. I'm sure my heart stopped beating for several seconds, that's how scared I was.

But it soon became evident that Roger had no thoughts of revenge.

"Rachel, you've got to help me!" he groaned. "They're after me – they're going to kill me!"

"But ... aren't you in Mexico?" I stammered. What an intelligent question, considering I could see with my own eyes that he was standing right in front of me in the hallway!

143

"They found out that I was hiding at your house. I don't know how they discovered me, but I had to get out of there quickly. I managed to get to my friend's house and thought for a while I might be safe there, but they found me again!"

"Who found you? I asked, bewildered. "What are you talking about?"

"They call themselves the Mexican Mob," he said, clearly distressed. "It was one of their gangs that was supposed to get the drugs that Will and I picked up."

"Did they follow you here, to the stable?" I asked with an anxious glance toward the slightly ajar door.

Roger followed my eyes, dashed over to the door and closed it properly. Then he came back to Núpur and me.

"I'm almost a hundred percent sure that I got away without them noticing," he said. "But with a little time I'm sure they'll track me down here, too."

"So you told the truth then, about Will," I whispered. "It wasn't you who shot him."

Roger shook his head. "I might as well tell you everything," he said and breathlessly proceeded to tell his story. It turned out that Bethany had been right in all of her speculations. Roger and Will had come in contact with a prison gang while they were in jail, and had found out about the planned plane drop of a big batch of drugs. Ignorant of just how dangerous the mobsters were, Roger and Will planned to snatch the drugs, in hopes of making some fast money. They had never intended to sell the drugs by themselves. They just wanted to collect a ransom for handing the stuff back to the intended recipients.

"At first we thought we'd arrived too late," said Roger. "We didn't manage to find our way to the drop site in time. So we decided to ask our friend to get us out of the country that same night. But then Will heard that the plane drop had been aborted, and he found out when the new attempt was going to take place."

Hence, Roger and Will had hidden in the woods and managed to snatch the packages right under the noses of the drug dealers. Unfortunately, they had totally underestimated their enemies. One of the gangsters had seen them before they got away with the packages, and later the gang got their hands on Will before he and Roger had a chance to even mention the word ransom. Will was forced to tell where the loot was hidden, and then they had *taken care* of him.

"But why are they still after you, if they have the drugs back?" I asked.

Apparently Roger and Will had been sneaky enough to hide the drugs in two different places. The gang members had only been told about one of them, so now they were after Roger to make him tell them where the rest of it was.

"Will and I thought we were so clever," he said, and it almost looked as if he was on the verge of tears. I actually started feeling a little sorry for him. "Clever indeed! Will is dead, and if they get their hands on me, I'll be a goner too. You have to help me, Rachel!"

"Me? How can I help you?" I said, confused. *And why should I?* I thought maliciously. But then I reconsidered. Regardless of what Roger had done, he didn't deserve to be killed.

"You have to call the police," said Roger.

I looked at him in disbelief.

"The police? But…"

"I'd rather be in jail, alive, than at the bottom of a lake with something heavy tied around my feet, don't you see?" moaned Roger, looking both miserable and pathetic now. There wasn't much left of the arrogant, sniggering Roger I had seen before.

"I'll go and call right away," I said quickly. "I'll just put Núpur in his stall first."

"Close the door when you leave," said Roger nervously.

I hurried outside, closing the door carefully behind me. Right then I wished there had been a phone in the stable, because I wasn't crazy about the idea of walking across the farmyard and over to the office. Glancing anxiously over my shoulder, I walked quickly. Was somebody there? No, everything seemed quiet and peaceful. I tried to calm down. Roger said he got away unnoticed, so it wasn't very likely that the gangsters would figured out where he'd gone for a while yet.

Bethany is not going to believe this – that Roger is actually begging to be picked up by the police, I thought, and couldn't help smiling at the idea. The whole thing was so unbelievable.

I was just about to open the door to the office, when I felt a hand on my shoulder, and a man's voice saying quietly, "Not a sound. Stay completely still."

I was in shock and automatically tried to turn around, but the hand stopped me and the voice said, "Don't turn around if you want to live."

I kept still, not moving a muscle, and felt drops of sweat forming on my forehead. My heart was beating so hard it made my ears buzz. It didn't take a genius to understand that Roger hadn't managed to slip away unseen after all. I was convinced that this was one of the Mob gang members.

"What are you going to do with me?" I whispered hoarsely. My legs shook so violently I thought I was going to collapse.

"First of all, make sure that you don't see my face," said the man. He had a dark, pleasant voice, which should have had a calming effect, but it didn't.

The man tied a scarf or something over my eyes and led me across the farmyard, keeping a firm grip on my shoulders.

"Just stay calm and do exactly as I say, and then nothing will happen to you," he said. "We're not interested in harming little kids."

For some reason I believed him. Maybe because the alternative was too horrible to consider. He led me through a doorway, and the familiar scent of hay and horse told me that we were in the stable.

"Did you stop her in time?" asked another unfamiliar voice.

"Yes, I caught her outside the door. Apparently she was going to call somebody," said my hostage taker. "I didn't have any problems with her."

"Smart girl," said the other man. "Tie her up and put her on the floor over there."

The man tied my hands behind my back and pushed me into a corner of the stable. Then he tied my ankles together. I was trembling. What would happen now? And where was Roger? I hadn't heard a sound from him. Was he captured already? The thought made me feel sick. But the next moment Roger talked. His voice was high-pitched and hysterical, "I'll tell you where the package is," he pleaded. "Just don't hurt me. Please!"

I shuddered. They weren't going to hurt Roger here in the stable, were they?

Instead I heard Roger keep pleading for mercy over and over again, "Please let me go. I'll never get in your way again."

The men laughed. "No, you're right about that," said one of them. "You'll never get in the way of anybody anymore. Come on now, we're going for a little drive."

Roger roared and made panic-stricken protests as the men, judging by the scraping and banging noises, maneuvered him toward the stable door.

I suddenly panicked myself. "What about me?" I shouted after them. "Aren't you going to untie me?"

"Sorry, we can't take the chance of letting you loose now and have you run straight to the police," said the man who had grabbed me outside. "We need a few hours to take care of things. I'm afraid you might have an uncomfortable night, but I assume people will be coming to the stable in the morning, right?"

"Yes," I said, meekly. I kept still, listening to the footsteps that were going away, and suddenly I remembered Bethany. I had forgotten about her during everything else that had happened. Where was she all this time? She should have been back by now. What if she ran right into the arms of the gangsters? What if she saw their faces? If so, they may not be content to simply tie her up, as they had done with me. What if...?

I heard the banging of car doors outside, and then suddenly a scraping sound on the stable door. Were the gangsters coming back? Had they changed their mind and decided to...?

"Rachel! Don't be scared, it's just me."

"Bethany?" I gasped. "I was so afraid that they might catch you too."

"No, they're leaving now," she said, pushing up my blindfold. I blinked at the bright light.

While Bethany struggled to loosen the knots on the rope I was tied with, we suddenly heard a lot of commotion outside. There were honking car horns and the sound of screeching brakes. Then we heard car doors being slammed and a lot of shouting and screaming.

"What on Earth is going on?" I asked, bewildered.

Bethany had a satisfied smile on her face.

"It sounds like the police made it just in time," she said. "Come on, let's have a look. Can you stand?"

"Yes, but..." I clambered to my feet and followed Bethany toward the stable door. The scene that greeted us in the farmyard

looked more like a Hollywood movie. Tough-looking police
– at least I assumed they were police, even though they weren't
wearing uniforms – were in the process of overpowering the two
gangsters, who I could now see for the first time. I was surprised
at how young they looked. My image of mobsters was fat,
middle-aged men in striped suits, but maybe they only look like
that in the movies. After a lot of pushing and shoving, where it
seemed like everyone was running in each other's way, three of
the policemen managed to push Roger and the two gangsters up
against a wall. It looked as if all three of them stopped resisting at
that point. A fourth policeman approached them with three sets of
handcuffs, and after their hands were cuffed behind their backs,
there wasn't much they could do anymore.

Even if it looked like the police had things under control
at that point, Bethany and I didn't dare to go outside. We
stood inside the stable doorway, watching through the door.
The police kept the three prisoners standing by the wall. It
looked as if they were waiting for something, and after a
while a big van with the word *Police* on the side showed up.
The three prisoners were loaded into the van, which then
drove away.

One of the policemen came over to us and asked if we were
both okay. He offered to drive us home, but we told him we
had to take care of the horses first, and that we could just bike
home. Now that the bad guys had been taken away, we felt safe
again. The policeman accepted this, and asked us to come by
the station the next day to give an eyewitness statement. He also
offered to arrange for post-traumatic therapy for me, since I'd
had such a scary experience, and I promised to think about it.

"By the way, I think it's the first time I've arrested someone
who was practically shouting for joy at being arrested," said
the policeman with a bemused smile. "Roger Soto pretty much

showered us with gratitude and thank yous when we took him away."

I had to laugh. "I'm not at all surprised that he was relieved," I said. "It wasn't exactly a Sunday picnic those two guys were planning for him!"

After the police left, I finally had a chance to ask Bethany, "How did you know that the police were coming?"

"Because I called them, of course," said Bethany triumphantly. "You see, on my way back from Martin's house – by the way, he wasn't home, so I left the note on his door   I saw a car driving up to the stable. It was rolling completely silently, so obviously the driver had turned off the engine. I thought it was kind of strange, but didn't really suspect something until I saw the two guys who stepped out of the cars. They definitely looked suspicious, and neither of them closed their door, as if they were trying very hard to not make any noise. I felt there was something wrong about the way they acted, and that they were doing everything they could to not be heard. At that point I didn't have a clue that Roger was in here. I thought you were alone, and I thought that the men might be horse thieves, or something like that. I was really scared for you."

I nodded. "Well, they definitely succeeded in not being heard," I said. "I didn't know a thing until one of them put his hand on my shoulder. I thought I was going to collapse from sheer fright."

"When I saw them grab you and take you into the stable, I quickly sneaked into the office and dialed 911," explained Bethany. "I told them that some guys were holding you prisoner in the stable and gave a description of the car and the two men I'd seen, and they promised me that the police would be here as fast as they could. And I must say – they were pretty fast!"

"You know, you probably saved Roger's life," I said quietly.

"I don't give a hoot about Roger!" said Bethany vehemently. "Well, of course I'm glad he's been arrested, but it was you I was worried about!" She threw her arms around me and hugged me tight.

"I'm so glad those creeps didn't hurt you," she exclaimed.

"And I'm at least as happy that they didn't hurt you," I said, hugging her back. "While I was sitting in there all tied up, I was *so* scared that you might run right into their arms and end up in a much worse situation than mine. Fortunately, the worst that could have happened to me was numb feet and a sore backside."

"Yeah – unless nature called, of course," said Bethany with a chuckle. Then she got serious again. "You should probably accept their offer to have some of that 'post-traumatic therapy' they mentioned," she said. "Otherwise you might start having nightmares about this for the rest of your life."

I nodded. "Mom accepted a similar offer after the robbery last year, and she said it helped a lot, so I'll probably do it, too. I have no desire to dream about Roger!" I laughed with a shiver.

"Gosh, no! I'd rather dream about rattlesnakes," said Bethany with a shudder.

"But I don't really want to dream about that either," I stated firmly. "The only things I want to dream about are horses – and one horse in particular."

I went into the stall where Núpur was standing, nodding his head drowsily. He peered at me with half-shut eyes. I put my arms around him and buried my face into his warm, thick mane. And while I stood there, listening to his calm breathing, I felt reassured that I would be able to put the nightmare behind me.

"From now on you and I are just going to enjoy ourselves," I mumbled quietly. "No more gangsters are going to make life miserable for us anymore, okay?"

"Amen to that!" said Bethany. "The rest of this summer vacation is going to be all about one thing, and one thing only..."

"Horses!" we both exclaimed simultaneously, and then we laughed.

"I'm already looking forward to our next ride," I whispered into Núpur's ear, and he snorted quietly as if he was saying that he did, too. A shiver of joy went through me. Tomorrow was going to be a wonderful day.